ALL WE NEED OF HELL

Books by Harry Crews

Gospel Singer
Naked in Garden Hills
This Thing Don't Lead to Heaven
Karate Is a Thing of the Spirit
Car
The Hawk Is Dying
The Gypsy's Curse
A Feast of Snakes
A Childhood
Blood and Grits
Florida Frenzy

All
We Need
of Hell

HARRY CREWS

HARPER & ROW, PUBLISHERS, New York

Cambridge, Philadelphia, San Francisco, Washington

1817   London, Mexico City, São Paulo, Singapore, Sydney

ALL WE NEED OF HELL. Copyright © 1987 by Harry Crews. All rights reserved.
Printed in the United States of America. No part of this book may be used or
reproduced in any manner whatsoever without written permission except in the case
of brief quotations embodied in critical articles and reviews. For information address
Harper & Row, Publishers, Inc., 10 East 53rd Street, New York, N.Y. 10022.
Published simultaneously in Canada by Fitzhenry & Whiteside Limited, Toronto.

Designer: Sidney Feinberg

Copy editor: Marjorie Horvitz

Library of Congress Cataloging-in-Publication Data

Crews, Harry, 1935–
  All we need of hell.

  I. Title.
PS3553.R46A74   1987   813'.54   86–45651
ISBN 0–06–015680–5

---

87 88 89 90 91 HC 10 9 8 7 6 5 4 3 2

This book is for Maggie Powell.

Mender of wings, restorer of flight, may you wheel and soar under the sun forever.

Parting is all we know of heaven,
And all we need of hell.

—Emily Dickinson

ALL WE NEED OF HELL

1

He was thinking of Treblinka. He had already finished with Dachau and Auschwitz. And now in an effort of will the images of death pumped in his head in a certain steady rhythm. Behind his pinched burning eyelids he saw a pile of frozen eyeglasses where they had been torn from the faces of long lines of men, women and children before they had been led into the gassy showers.

"Daddy. Please, daddy. I love . . . love . . . love. But it hurts."

Her whispering voice impinged upon the images of death. He shook it off and concentrated on open pits of lime-covered bodies. Not even people anymore. Rather manikins out of some bankrupt department store. Starved to the point of caricature. But once men and women. Once somebody not unlike himself. He imagined himself in the shower. In the pit. In the slave-labor gangs.

"You're killing me."

Yes, and by God he would. He'd kill. He'd do anything. He would become a proficient murderer and thief. He saw his wasted, tragic figure stealing along in the shadows of death-camp barracks. He saw in his hands a single strand of thin wire, the death instrument.

"Please. Please *come*."

Her hands were moving over his body. Stroking, pinching, caressing, probing. And she was begging. He had her where he wanted her. He had brought her to the place of pain and punishment. He relaxed his thighs, forced the muscles in his lower back to go flaccid.

She was kissing his closed eyes, begging him to look at her. But he gripped his eyes tighter. He knew that trick. She'd only show him the deep pink inside her mouth. Make her tongue stand and work like a snake. So he shut out her voice and her body by slipping the garrote around the neck of a fellow prisoner and stealing his half-eaten potato. The prisoner's gaspy choking breath mixed with her breath, became her breath. And the prisoner's starving body entered her thrusting, magnificent thighs. He killed her where he rode her, there on the high crest of his passion. And when she was dead he twisted the half-eaten moldy potato out of her hand.

"I guess you're too young to remember Pathé News," he said.

They were through now. He was putting on his bicycle racing hat. Marvella lay exhausted on the bed. He had made her cry. But she was still beautiful. As always, he was vaguely insulted that she should remain so utterly beautiful after he had given her such pain, such a beating.

"Pathé News," she said, her voice numb with exhaustion.

He could taste the moldy potato in his mouth. In the mirror, the red stripe on his hard bicycle racing hat was tilted at a cocky angle. He watched her in the mirror, her bemused gaze balancing delicately in his own. He tried to look savage.

"We used to get the news at the neighborhood movie," he said. "They told us everything. I loved it." He had his jockstrap on now—a number ten medium—and was stepping into a pair of blue nylon shorts. She sat up in bed and watched him. "One disaster after another. Burning blimps. Collapsing buildings. Ships blowing up."

"It musta been something," Marvella said.

2

He sat on the edge of the bed and began lacing his blue leather Adidas shoes onto his feet. His eyes were still full of dying children and hopeless parents. He did not have to listen to hear the sound of the begging voices.

"The greatest was when they liberated the concentration camps."

He stood up and rolled on the balls of his feet.

"My grandmother was German," she said.

"Great organizers, the Germans," he said. "They had that whole country set up to kill."

"And it was on the Pathé News?"

"Every bit of it on Saturday afternoons."

She watched him absently for a long moment and wondered in her heart what they had been talking about. There were whole afternoons when they would talk without her ever knowing what he was trying to say, or trying to get her to say maybe. There had been times at first when she had tried to get him to explain.

"Sure," he would say, "it's just this simple."

Then he'd say something that made no sense at all, which did not bother her but infuriated him. It was in a way relaxing, though, because she never had to pay attention.

"Saturdays were always cartoon time at my house," she said.

He turned angrily from his bicycle where it leaned against the closet door. "What?"

"We watched cartoons on TV all day on Saturday."

He looked down at the bicycle chain he was locking around his waist. Ten pounds of the finest tempered steel. He was suddenly baffled. He had a three-hundred-dollar bicycle that weighed seventeen pounds. And a twenty-five-dollar chain that weighed ten. The bicycle was so expensive because it was so light. But because it was so expensive he had to have a heavy chain, one that would require a torch to cut. There were, after all, thieves in the world. And consequently everything seemed to cancel everything else out. But the relationship was not consequential. And he knew it. Thieves had nothing to do with it. He looked up and saw that she had started to chew gum in her slow contented beautiful way.

"Well . . . well." He was beside himself with anger. "Well, to hell with it!"

Not a ripple of anything showed in her face. She just kept on chewing as he rolled his bicycle out into the middle of the room.

"You're probably right," she said, getting off the bed. She took an apple from a dish by the window. "I could have used my mind better than that."

He watched her in a kind of ecstasy of loathing. The pearling window light cast her body long and delicious. Her pink tongue brought the gum wetly into her hand. Her white teeth shattered the apple. Little shards of juice flew brightly from her mouth. A tremble ran in his legs where the blood pumped. He knew her addiction to soap operas on afternoon TV. And she not only collected science fiction novels; she also read them. She enjoyed them. She said they made her think, which meant she was dumb in the gravest kind of way. Duffy himself was addicted to reading and in the constant company of books. But he never read science fiction, which he thought of as chewing gum for the mind.

She was also a Woodrow Wilson Fellow in the Philosophy Department at the University of Florida. It was said that she had the single most brilliant graduate record ever made in the history of the department. But only something very dumb could chew gum like that. Only the most brutal kind of ignorance could talk the way she did. He couldn't prove it. He just knew it. It was all mixed together in there then, her graduate record and her bovine dumbness. The heavy chain and the light bicycle all over again.

"You coming back?" she said.

"Can't you remember any fucking thing?"

"Remember?"

"Yes. Remember."

"What?"

"Jesus," he said.

"Duffy, you say the strangest old thangs."

Duffy sighed. "To answer your question, no, I'm not coming back. Not today anyway."

"When you think?" She may be a Woodrow Wilson Fellow, but she had never completely lost the cadences of Alabama, where they named their daughters things like Marvella. And even better, she had a brother named Roid. Duffy had heard her talk about him for a long time before he realized that she was not saying *Roy*. He asked her to spell it for him. She had. *Roid*, for God's sake. Was that an affectionate diminutive for hemorrhoid? He decided that it probably was. But even if it wasn't, what a wonderful thing for a brother and sister to be named Marvella and Roid. And to be from Alabama. The rest of the country may have been homogenized, but the South held on to their Marvellas and their Roids and their ways of talking. Marvella would never sound like a goddam radio announcer. He could love her for that. That if for nothing else.

"When you think?" she said again.

"Probably a week, maybe two. Whenever we get back to town."

"I forgot. You're taking Tish and the kid on a little vacation."

Christ, he thought, she's going to eat another fucking apple, her third. She drove Tish's name through the red skin, into the seedy core. A little froth of spittle and juice stood in the corner of her indifferent mouth.

"She and the boy may not go with me. But I'm sure as hell going." He was doing rapid knee bends on his bowed, muscled legs. He was bored with the conversation. He could feel the handball and gloves throbbing in his back pocket. His own palms were turning hot, smarting where they rested lightly on the taped handlebars. He slipped his tinted goggles down off his bicycle racing hat. The room darkened from behind the goggles. She stood by the window, a purple shadow with white chewing teeth.

"Tish still giving you a hard time, is she?" She spat the pulpy

5

core into her hand and popped the chewing gum back into her mouth.

"Leave Tish out of this."

"I wish to goodness we could," Marvella said. "Tish doesn't know a good thing when she's got it."

Duffy said: "Tish knows exactly what she's got."

"Then I don't see the problem."

"Nobody's satisfied," he said, pushing his bike to the door.

"I guess not," she said.

He stopped at the door. "Actually I think Hitler was satisfied, at least there for a while," he said, not looking at her. "But even if they hadn't stopped him, he would've run out of Jews and Gypsies sooner or later."

"Hitler was a beast," she said. "An evil beast."

Duffy turned on her, his face flushing in anger. "Save that shit for somebody else. My daddy fought the bastard. He flew twenty-seven goddam missions before . . ."

"Duffy, don't start with My Father the Pilot. Not now."

He was suddenly calm. "Right. Not now. Not ever again. It's all wasted on you anyway."

2

He lifted the bike with one hand and opened the door with the other. With the crossbar of that sweet machine over his shoulder, he sprinted down five flights of outside stairs—outside even though this was a modern apartment house of neo-Aztec design that passed for elegance here in Gainesville, Florida, all angles and rough edges of poured cement—down the stairs to the street. The morning was brilliant, so blue that the air shimmered with palpable intensity.

The deserted Sunday streets were heated up, wavering, becoming unsubstantial under a sun that rode his back like a weight. He hesitated at the curb, feeling good, his skin popping with a thin sweat. The bicycle under his hands felt brittle as the bones of a sparrow. He let the alloy frame come into his wrists and forearms, move to his shoulders and back, while he stood very still, safe behind the tinted goggles, safe in the hard pulsing body he had built as deliberately and carefully as a mason builds a wall. His hard supple ankles rolled delicately under pointed calves that melded in a single flow of muscle to thighs that could do ten deep squats with three hundred pounds, exactly twice his body weight. His legs wanted the bicycle. If they had a voice they would have screamed for it.

Then, in a movement like a bird taking flight, he saddled

7

the bicycle with himself. His feet went true to the stirrups, strapped in tight and sure; his calloused hands took the taped grips; his narrow rocklike buttocks did not so much sit as lean on the leather seat. He was balanced on three points of equal weight—hands, feet, buttocks—and his begoggled face, grinning madly, split the air. The thick black hair curling from under the helmet stood straight behind him like a banner. He shot up through the gears to tenth and back down to his cruising gear, seventh.

Now he set himself to possess the bicycle, possess it all over again, each time a new time, and dangerous in what it cost him, but not because he might get hurt. He had been hurt doing everything he had ever done. He expected it, even wanted it. Nothing centered a man like pain. Nothing drove the irrelevant bullshit out of your mind like the taste of your own blood. Duffy always wanted to tell people who were worried about the future of their children, or about God and the order of the universe, to go out and break a rib or two. A few broken ribs threw all thoughts of children, God and the order of the universe right out the window. Nobody with broken ribs ever had free-floating anxiety, or so Duffy was convinced. It was cheaper than a psychiatrist and never so humiliating.

He was riding a handmade Gitane Tour De France ten-speed touring machine with an enclosed Simplex derailleur and hand-sewn paper-thin racing tires that went flat every night and had to be pumped up every morning. The tires, like everything else about the Gitane, were an inconvenience he suffered in order to ride the best. The rims were not steel but an alloy, and therefore lighter than steel but at the same time more likely to be damaged by rocks and holes in the road. But no matter, steel was too heavy. Alloy meant speed, maneuverability, so he tried to avoid rocks and holes with the sure and certain knowledge that sooner or later he would not be able to, and consequently ruin the bike and himself. But it would *not* be consequential. That was what he knew. Sooner or later the bike would be ruined. It had nothing to do with rocks and holes. What it had to do with was the fact that the world was a very dangerous place for any living thing, a simple self-evident truth that everyone Duffy had ever known had tried to deny. Except his father. Anytime Duffy cared to listen, he could hear his father's hoarse, beseeching voice: "Embrace what cannot be changed. Hug it to yourself and make it your own." Duffy had taken him at his word and embraced the world with a vengeance, or at least he hoped that he had.

The gearshifts were not on the crossbar, as they were on other bikes. He had modified it so that the gear for the front two-speed sprocket was at the left end of the handlebar and the gear for the back five-speed sprocket was at the right end of the handlebar. That way his hands never had to move when he was sprinting. Without ever leaving the taped grips, he worked the gearshifts with his little fingers. He let both little fingers touch the gears now although he did not mean to shift. He only wanted to make himself feel the taut thin steel cables humming down the handlebars and down the angled crossbar and down the joining H bar to the Simplex derailleur. He did not want himself and the Gitane (feminine form of the French word for Gypsy) to be separate. As he did before a karate match, he let his mind fill with light, the source of which was invisible, a slightly blue room covered with mirrors reflecting nothing. He always used techniques from one art to inform another art.

"A man doesn't have twenty different disciplines, or thirty-five, or a hundred," he often told his son. "It is all one discipline. A solid tempered thing at the center of a man that is indestructible. The mystery that keeps you alive if you've got it, or that lets you die if you don't."

The girl was an art every bit as much as karate or cycling. Fucking was just another workout. But because it was didn't mean it couldn't be raised to the level of art. Any craft could. It only required knowledge and concentration. He often thought fucking ought to be included in the Olympics. Judged on difficulty and variety of positions and how smoothly the positions were integrated. The ultimate dance. Nothing could be faked.

When the judge clapped his hands and cried: *At the ready! Set! Penetrate!* you either had it up or you were disqualified. A live audience of seventy thousand people and millions more on world television would watch as the sheep were separated from the goats. A million suburban husbands, jaded, potbellied, a cold beer by the chair, would watch with their hearts in their throats. And he, absolutely poised and ready, would bring them to their feet with his performance. Only victory, winning in the moment, made the knowledge of ultimate failure and death bearable. It often occurred to him that it was all probably meaningless anyway, a kind of game. But if it took a game to keep him alive, so be it. Whatever was necessary was necessary. Again, he could hear the mad voice of his father: "I'm alive, am I not? Alive!" Duffy would do anything to win, just as he had this morning with Marvella.

He hadn't meant to think of the Nazis and their experiments in death. But he had felt himself on the edge of coming, and the mountain of frozen eyeglasses popped into his head. The wonderful images of death. The gas. The screams. And he knew she would not beat him. He'd take her where he wanted her to go. But not without a price. All the trouble he had gone to to have that twenty-two-year-old girl locked up with him, only to find she had brought a corpse with her. A girl for his body and a corpse for his head. Everything canceled everything else out. It was a situation he thought he could understand and that struck him as nothing more than a commonplace.

And he was left with what he was always left with: his body's enthusiasm. It was all he ever felt safe with. You could, after all, measure that, understand the failure, control the performance. If you were willing to pay the price you could make your body do anything. Nobody knew what it could be made to do. Hadn't everybody assumed that a four-minute mile was impossible? And when Roger Bannister's body paid the price, how long did his fact, his record, stand? Seventeen days. Less than three weeks later another man's body, with four stopwatches on it, produced its own miracle and there went poor old Roger down the drain. Now there was not a class miler in the world who didn't own a four-minute mile. Discipline. Price. The body's enthusiasm. That was probably where God lived, in a hot muscle strained beyond its limits.

He was passing a Volkswagen now. Out of the sides of his tinted goggles he saw the startled driver blink in disbelief. He held his body in a perfect wind scoop, head low, eyes just above the handlebars, back flat across the shoulders and rising to the curve that the wind passed over and then pushed against, knees very tight, only the width of the crossbar apart.

His legs were beginning to talk back to him now. There was not a joint in his body that did not ache. Something sharp that he had not felt before, like a knife cutting, was pushing between his ribs on the right side. He deliberately worked the right side harder, pulling with the right hand, pushing with the right thigh. He was on a long, slightly downhill sprint that took him by the handball courts. His speed, he thought, was right at forty. He always shot by once without stopping, to intimidate the players. It usually stopped play on half the courts. None of them had ever seen a bicycle go forty miles an hour before. He kept his head down and didn't look, never broke his stride or form, but in his peripheral vision he saw the blurred line of players staring.

Just as he was past the courts, but still where he knew they could see him, he turned loose the handlebars and stood straight up in the stirrups, both arms raised, fists clenched. He had once broken both collarbones and fractured his skull standing up like that. But at this speed it was beautiful enough to be worth the risk.

Let them look upon him and despair. They were about to be thrashed, cut down, humiliated. He could almost hear them groan. Duffy Deeter had done it again, swooped over the Sunday handball courts like a hawk over chickens. He eased back onto the saddle of the Gitane, took the taped grips, applied a judicious brake, and coasted back to the courts. Still not looking at the players, he carefully leaned his bike against the chain-link fence and, even though he'd never be out of sight of it, unlocked the ten-pound chain from around his hips. He ran the chain through the back wheel, frame, sprocket and fence before he fastened it with the special lock, which itself weighed eighteen ounces. He straightened up, unstrapped the bicycle racing hat, lifted it off with the goggles, and dropped it on the ground under the stirrups. Then he stripped off his sweat-soaked pullover shirt. He draped the shirt from the brake grip and walked casually out onto the court.

He saw Jert McPhester leaning against the water fountain by the first court. Jert was his law partner and the last person he wanted to see, which made Duffy feel he had to go directly to him and made him wish he could stand eyeball-to-eyeball with him. But Jert was six feet six inches tall and had anchored the defensive end position of the University of Florida at a playing weight of two hundred and thirty-five pounds. Everything about him was huge; even his head seemed monstrous under a thick mat of springy, tightly curled blond hair. When Duffy stood too close to Jert it made him feel as if he was surrounded, because Jert didn't so much stand as he loomed.

"Jert."

"Duffy."

They watched a slender left-handed player who really was not very good at all kill the ball at the baseline.

"Luck," said Jert.

Duffy moved out of Jert's shadow and said: "It never hurts to have a little."

"We didn't seem to have much luck on Friday," said Jert.

Jert laughed the sudden nervous laugh that meant he was angry enough to hit something. Duffy had blown a hundred-thousand-dollar whiplash case on Friday. Or at least Friday had been the day the jury came in and said his client wasn't getting a cent. Even though they had seen it coming for more than a week, nobody believed it. They'd had the insurance company dead on the line and Duffy had somehow managed to blow it. The lady, his client, had sat there stunned, unable to look at him because she could not move her disastrously whiplashed neck. The jury of course had concluded that she was faking.

"I didn't expect to see you here today," said Duffy, trying to get off the subject of Friday.

"Too hot for golf," Jert said. "Besides, I wanted to show you something."

What Jert was showing him right then was his belly. He had his Banlon golfing shirt pulled up and he was staring at his belly, gingerly probing it with his thick football fingers. Jert often stared at his belly, as though genuinely surprised—shocked maybe— to find it growing there. He had been an All-American as a sophomore but in his senior year he had earned not All-American or even All-Conference, but had earned zippers on his knees instead, and now the All-American who would have been All-Pro spent his leisure time walking around on a golf course or watching his belly grow. He was thirty pounds over playing weight. All belly. Still, Duffy had to agree with his wife, Tish: Jert was a strikingly good-looking sonofabitch. Being six feet six inches tall, he could carry thirty pounds of belly. In a nation of generally overfed people, only another jock would even notice it hanging on him.

Duffy watched him probing his stomach. "How's it feel in there?"

Color ran in Jert's thick neck. "A little belly, sure." He patted it with false affection. "But I can still bust ass."

Duffy thought: What you mean, you mountain of flab, is that you'd like to bust *my* ass. All for losing the lousy forty percent of the lousy hundred thou of a lousy lead-tight cinch that any freshman in law school could have won.

"It's good to see you out here," said Jert. "Get your blood pumping, more oxygen to the old brain. The old brain does not function well running on an oxygen deficit."

"I wouldn't deny that things have been a little loose for me lately," said Duffy. "After I get away with the family for a while in the camper, I'll be all put back together."

"Tish and Felix actually going with you?"

Duffy watched him quietly. "Why wouldn't they be going with me?"

"Just a guess. Frankly, Duffy, I've been expecting Tish to give you the shuck."

"Jert, you really ought to stay the fuck out of my personal life."

"Just an observation."

"I don't need your observations."

"How's little Felix getting on?"

"Leave it alone, Jert."

"You seem so jangled—ill at ease—around your son, and I was just wondering. . . ."

"Don't wonder. I'll take care of me and mine."

"There's no reason to be so defensive. Have you been into something I ought to know about?"

"Just your old mother."

A vein forked in Jert's forehead. "Someday you'll go too far, Duffy."

Duffy turned on his heel, giving his back to Jert and whipping his handball gloves out of his back pocket. "To hell with this. I came out here to get a game."

"Listen, I brought a guy who might give you a workout," said Jert.

His voice was so offhand and casual that Duffy knew immediately something good and awful was about to happen. He stopped in the burning sun, his back still to Jert. He stood there drawing on his thin nylon gloves, which had no padding in them at all. Padding kept you from feeling the ball. It put something between you and the game you were playing. His hands came alive with a feeling that was always new and exquisite the instant he stuffed them into the musky sweat-soaked dankness of a pair of handball gloves. Jert had come up beside him now. Duffy flexed his hands, took the ball out of his pocket, bounced it hard, sliced it with bottom inside English when it came by his face so fast that nobody saw the ball, and it looped high and back over his left shoulder, dropping into the opposite pocket. It wasn't

14

much of a trick. Given perfect reflexes and coordination and a lot of practice, any really first-class circus juggler could have done it.

"Always up for a little game," said Duffy. As he spoke he felt the sharp stab of pain between the lower ribs on his right side. He figured he must have torn a muscle on the girl that morning. After he got inside the concentration camp to help him, to give staying power, he must have worked out on her for an hour and a half. No matter. He'd suck it up and go.

Jert had put a meaty hand on his shoulder. "He's around on the other side of the wall. Court's better over there, sun won't be in your eyes."

Jert was just so chatty it made him want to throw up. Duffy hadn't lost a game of singles in nearly two years. He had not in fact lost a game since Florida's offensive line coach Tater Medders died of a heart attack. Since then he had been undisputed king of the courts. So whatever was making Jert—whom Duffy knew to be suffering badly over the forty thousand the partnership had lost on Friday—so hand-on-your-shoulder and we-don't-want-the-sun-in-your-eyes friendly had to be root-hog mean and ugly. Duffy saw the audience first. Probably twenty-five handball players were sitting or standing by the high chain-link fence staring without moving, without appearing to blink.

3   Duffy turned the corner at the high wall and saw
what they saw. That he was root-hog mean there could be no
doubt, but ugly he was not. He had on white handball shoes,
white gloves, white shorts, white head and wrist sweatbands, all
of it over a blue-black skin alive with muscles of awesome sym-
metry. He almost had the cuts between muscles, the definition,
that Duffy had. But not quite. Duffy had the thinnest skin in
the world and muscles that were trained and sharpened from,
among other things, fifty-mile bike tours in a rubberized sweat
suit.

"Hey, Tump, this is the guy I was telling you about," called
Jert.

The black guy, who had been gently pushing the ball against
the wall, doing little three-cornered billiard angles with it, stopped
and walked over to the baseline where they were standing. Across
the left leg of his white shorts was written *Philadelphia Eagles*.
But Duffy knew he didn't play for them anymore. They had
traded him to the Miami Dolphins. The Dolphins had given up
a first-round draft choice and an undisclosed sum of cash for this
man, this Tump Walker.

"Tump Walker, this is Duffy Deeter," said Jert. "Duffy,
Tump."

"I've seen you work," said Duffy. "And you do real good, Tump."

"Jert says you shoot a little handball," said Tump. "That's what he says."

"I play some from time to time." Duffy put a little cut in his voice and looked away, giving them the sarcastic back of his head.

"I been told," Tump said.

"I guess we *could* just stand around out here in the sun and talk it to death," said Duffy Deeter.

He was really feeling feisty now. Just knowing Jert had set it up (although he didn't know what *it* was yet) made Duffy's whole body begin to sing. He wanted to get hurt, to have some pain put on himself, just so he could come back from it, just so he could suck it up and go. Duffy at least partially knew the reason for Jert being here this morning. Jert was a big team jock, and had gone to seed as only a team jock can. Duffy had never played a team sport in his life, and yet at forty, he was still lean and mean and good. He could give you four five-thirty minute miles back-to-back. Or rappel down a thousand feet of sheer rock. Or run white water alone without a life preserver. Or drink straight sour mash whiskey for twenty hours straight. He even entered the rodeo in Ocala every year. Riding bulls. He had, goddammit, *enthusiasm*.

They had tested the balls and found the one with the most life (it was Duffy's) and were now throwing to the line to see who served first. There was not another game in progress anymore on the other twenty courts. A solid bank of players lined the fence, as silent as if they had been in church. Just how good Tump was showed when he threw the ball for serve. He didn't even appear to look, just sort of nonchalantly banked it off the back wall and still only missed the line by a quarter inch. But Duffy hit it. Squarely. Tump smiled.

"Serve it up, my man," said Tump.

Tump never even saw it. Duffy brought it off the left wall with so much top English on it that the ball squeaked and left a mark, came back to right court, then diagonally across the left again, where Tump still stood flat-footed. A little groan came out of the handball players ranged against the fence. Duffy smiled back at Tump.

"My slow one," he said.

"Un huh," said Tump.

It had been twenty-three straight games since anybody had taken a serve away from Duffy. If he got the ball on the bounce, that was the first game. But Tump was much better than he looked on that first serve. He brought back a left-handed three-wall smash, and then came to center court, where he used his size to dominate play, and on the third return of the volley, he broke serve. Duffy didn't mind Tump using his size. Everybody plays the center of the court. And you use whatever advantage you have. A few shoulders, a few hips. Always playing to the other man's disadvantage. But that was not exactly what Tump was doing. He was hunting for Duffy's head. On the second return of the volley Duffy knew the name of the game; it was called take Duffy out *bad*. Hurt him. Aggression and deliberate malice was coming off Tump now like heat off a stove. Besides whatever deal Tump may have had with Jert, Duffy knew what was really hurting Tump was that he was in imminent danger of being beaten badly by a little man in front of a big crowd.

But even though he sensed what was about to happen, Duffy never saw the lick coming. Because he *was* quick, Tump Walker was. Hummingbird hands and feet. They were at center court. Very tight with each other, hip to hip. Duffy hit a high lob shot and started back to be in a position to return. But Tump didn't even wait for the ball to come off the wall. He did it with the back of his open hand. He must have been watching Duffy's head instead of the ball, because he really had the range. He didn't even look. The blow took Duffy entirely off his feet, turning him once in the air, and once on the ground. He was out momentarily, everything black and swimming. But instinct and long training brought him to his feet. He would have come to his feet if his leg had been broken, as in fact he once had at a karate tournament.

He felt rather than saw Tump's heavy arms around him, steadying him. Jert's belly was pressing into his back. Voices babbled. The darkness was going, his head was clearing.

". . . sorry, little brother," said Tump. "Man, I'm *real* sorry."

Duffy put his hand to his lips. Blood. He felt something under his tongue. A tooth. He blew it out of his mouth. Another tooth was broken diagonally across; it hurt his tongue to touch it. And it was all Duffy could do to keep himself from taking Tump's head off right there. But they were playing a certain game by certain rules. It sure as hell wasn't handball, but it was nonetheless a game. And he meant to play it out.

"It's all right," he said. "Just one of those things that happen. Hit the ball."

"But, little brother, you bleeding."

"I know it was an accident." He spat blood. "Hit the ball."

"You sure you can play?"

"I can play."

But he had no intention of playing. Not handball anyway. When Tump served, Duffy went up for the ball, his entire body lying out parallel to the ground—five feet above it—and delivered a perfectly executed Okinawan roundhouse reverse, leading with the heel of his right foot, to Tump's head—the back of it—and also returned the ball in a three-walled zinger that Tump could not have returned even if he had not already collapsed on the court like a sack of wet laundry.

There was sudden and total silence on the court. Tump lay quietly bleeding from the nose and mouth where his face had struck the cement. An ugly knot—slightly red even through the black skin—was growing at the base of his skull. Duffy looked carefully at the knot, to observe the accuracy of the kick, and saw that he had missed the center of the cortex by at least a quarter of an inch. He made a note to himself to do an extra hour's work with the mackawari board.

Jert finally found his voice and came screaming onto the court. "You've killed him, you vicious bastard. You've *killed* him."

"Tell'm when he comes to," Duffy said, "that he shoots a pretty good game. But tell'm it's too bad he couldn't go the distance."

He strolled away from their unbelieving eyes, got on his bike and pushed off gently down University Avenue. As he was leaving he could hear Jert shouting what a lousy human being he was. Duffy tried to smile. But he couldn't quite make it. The world did seem to be getting a tight place to live in. A man couldn't seem to find any slack anywhere. Or at least *he* couldn't. And when you can't find slack, you're through. Everything he'd ever seen in the world pointed to that.

Corpses to keep fucking. Kicking guys in the head to stay alive at handball. Confusing times. The whiplash case he had lost was an ordinary example of his extraordinary state of mind. Or not of mind, of being.

He thought he would take about ten miles at about twenty per before going home, which he dreaded because he knew the corpses to keep fucking and the extraordinary violence of his life and all the rest of it were rooted there in his house with a wife and child he could not understand, that he could not live with. He thought of the last couch Tish had bought. He had come home from the office and his wife had bought another couch, a real monster, black, covered in deep velvet, and twelve feet long. It drove him unreasonably crazy. His living room, and it was a huge room, was so jammed with furniture and lamps and every manner of stuffed and carved chair that it reminded him of a furniture showroom.

"Jesus, Tish," he said.

"McDougal's was having a sale."

"*Four* couches, for God's sake? There's one for me, one for you and one for the boy. Who's the fourth one for?"

"McDougal's only sells quality merchandise. And this was a bargain."

She was plucking her eyebrows in front of a huge oval-shaped mirror propped on the heavy mahogany coffee table in front of her. She had not looked up. He sometimes thought he'd smother in the house, filled as it was with the bounty of her daily raids on stores of every kind. He felt himself drowning in a sea of things. He couldn't remember exactly when she started packing the house in this unseemly way.

"You need a hobby, Tish," he said. "Or maybe even a job. You've got too much time on your hands."

She examined one thin, arching eyebrow more closely in the mirror. "I've been thinking of trying my hand at interior decorating."

She might as well have said that she had been thinking of trying her hand at brain surgery. He rushed into the kitchen and drank a quart of skim milk mixed with protein powder and garlic.

He had the twenty-mile-an-hour rhythm now. He settled down to let his legs hold it, and consciously made himself think about the fiasco in court to keep his mind off going home to Tish. He had always known that a jury trial was a contest of contending liars. Because even if lawyers don't know what the truth is, they do know that the superstructure of words they are putting together, the *image* they are forcing to take shape there in the courtroom, is a lie. A lie because each side's view is diametrically opposed and no two things are diametrically opposed. Perhaps not provable, but every man with a brain knows that. So the best liar, the most cogent liar, wins. Hell, Duffy had always known that. It's the cornerstone of every law school in the nation. That wasn't the trouble in the whiplash case. Not the trouble at all.

The trouble was confusion. Duffy's. He was used to every witness telling a different story. Sometimes stories so radically different that they could not possibly have to do with the same phenomenon. That was just courtroom reality. But you always knew that *something* had happened though, because you always had a dead body or a burned building or a certifiably forged signature or, as in this case, a lady who could not turn her head.

But as this case proceeded—and it lasted nearly nine full trial days—Duffy, for the first time in his experience as a lawyer, became convinced that nothing *did* happen. There was no wreck. As the witnesses paraded to the stand and told their stories, their versions, things began to disappear. The street corner where it was supposed to have happened, a corner Duffy had walked and measured himself, disappeared under the weight of cross-examination of the lawyers and under the weight of the crossed visions of the witnesses. The car, with its crushed rear end, was next to go as mechanics and police experts and insurance adjusters converged at the stand to say how it must have happened, whether the car was in motion or at rest when struck, how hard it was struck, if perhaps the dented and banged-up rear end was not the evidence of an *old* wreck and not in fact struck this time at all. Next the doctors came and they were the worst of the lot. They had probed with their fingers. But they all had different fingers and their different fingers felt something different. They had taken X-rays, but my God, the vague smudges they found significant were incomprehensible to everybody else in the courtroom because each doctor found them significant for a variety of reasons, none of them the same, and all directed toward a different medical conclusion. So the lady's neck disappeared next. She obviously did not have a neck.

It scared the hell out of Duffy. He spent all the recesses doing push-ups. He quit even talking to his client and just did push-ups and sit-ups and walked on his hands round and round the conference table where he should have been having strategy talks with the poor lady who could not move her neck.

The ride out Millhopper Road calmed him some, and by the time he got back onto Tenth Avenue he was feeling much better. He was cooling out now, not sprinting, just sitting straight up on the seat, riding without hands at a lazy relaxed rhythm. He was determined not to think anymore about the whiplash case or how it had affected him. What the hell, anybody was apt to get a little freaky once in a while. Your head was a funny place. Anybody's was. Duffy knew it. He prided himself on knowing that. And when something freaky came into it, you went with it. Or if you didn't go with it, you sure as hell didn't worry about it. All of it was you. That was what Zen taught. And hadn't Laotse, centuries before Zen was created, said: "Those who justify themselves do not convince." He didn't have to justify anything. And wouldn't. If the lady's neck disappeared, it disappeared. If those conflicting voices caused the entire courtroom to ultimately drop from view, so what? It would reappear. All things can happen. And have. And will again.

He got off the bike at the street and pushed it down the long circular drive leading to his house, past the enclosed heated swimming pool, past his enormous camper, which was all packed and ready to go. Walking down this drive toward his house, he sometimes felt as if he were walking to his execution. Not always, but sometimes. This morning was one of them. He felt something dying in him every step he took. He thought it was because he could never seem to get in step with his family. Never strike a balance that he could bear. Or they could bear, for that matter.

That wasn't true, he told himself. There had been a time when he was at one with his family. The balance was there. Where had it gone? How had he become so separated from . . . from, well, *separated*. When he had been locked up with Marvella that morning, doing the friendliest thing two people can do, she might as well have been in Europe and he in Tierra del Fuego. Somewhere along the way he had made a wrong turn, walked out of a rain forest onto a desert. Sand stretched away to all his horizons, and he was without direction. But if he kept walking long enough and pressed hard enough, he told himself, he would force his life to some conclusion.

4

His son was sitting in front of the house, on the lawn. He had something in his hand. Duffy knew before he got there that it was candy. Eleven o'clock on a Sunday morning and the kid was eating candy. The boy looked up and saw him coming down the drive. He lifted his soft pudgy hand. He didn't wave, he only lifted his hand and let it fall listlessly back into his lap. Then he tore the paper farther down the candy bar and took another bite. Duffy was close enough to see what it was. A Baby Ruth, one of the king-sized, quarter-pound numbers. It made Duffy's stomach tight with nausea.

"Come on in the back, son," Duffy said, without looking at the boy because he didn't want to see the candy bar again. "Finish up there and come on back. We ought to meditate awhile."

The boy got up like an old man, full of sighs and grunts. At nine years old and ninety pounds, the boy was probably no more than ten pounds overweight, but he was so utterly flabby and without grace that he appeared thirty pounds too heavy. And unlike Duffy, he never tanned. He got that from his mother. She was nearly a goddam albino. Beautiful to be sure, but even her pussy was white. Before Duffy met her, he had never even seen a blond pussy, much less a white one. It was probably why he married her, he often thought. When he saw that strange, wondrous pad of hair, he had to have it for his own. He was like that. Another form of his enthusiasm. Well, better enthusiasm than *nothing*.

Tish was sitting on the couch from McDougal's surrounded by a jungle of other furniture. The blinds and curtains were drawn, the house hermetically sealed, and the air conditioner turned up full blast. Duffy picked his way into the room through a narrow path of chairs and lamps and end tables. He could feel the sweat drying on his back and chest. Goose bumps prickled his thighs, still hot from the ride.

"You've got it cold enough in here to keep hamburger," he said.

She did not look up or even appear to be breathing there where she sat in a pair of purple hot pants and a see-through net blouse. She looked like an advertisement out of one of the wretched magazines she subscribed to. Her silver hair was piled high in an elaborate design that he knew must have taken at least an hour of her time that morning. He also knew it was hard as a rock under about half a can of some dreadful spray. Mess around all morning with her hair and give the boy a Baby Ruth for breakfast. Well, the good with the bad. That's who she was. Had not Confucius said that it was better to be human-hearted than righteous. She was only human-hearted, Duffy told himself, not believing it and gritting his teeth until his mouth hurt.

She had a cup of steaming black coffee beside her and had begun putting bright red polish on her nails. Her beautiful feet were in cork-wedged, high-heeled house slippers. She waved her hand slowly on the air and then stared at her thumb intently for what seemed to Duffy an unforgivably long time.

"I said, 'It's cold enough to keep hamburger in here.' "

She finally looked at him, but for all that showed in her face, he might as well have been another piece of furniture she was looking over.

"Hamburger?" she said.

"Right."

"You want it now?"

"What?"

"You'll have to cook it yourself."

"Cook what?"

"The hamburger."

"You know I don't eat that greasy shit."

"Then why'd you ask for it?"

"Jesus Christ."

"Don't start on that, Duffy."

"On what?"

"That."

"Hamburger?"

She sighed and looked at the ceiling. "What's come over you, Duffy?"

Duffy started to answer and then checked out the ceiling himself. It seemed like a good question. He wished to hell he had an answer for it.

"You going to be long there?"

"Where?"

"Doing your nails."

"Only until I finish."

"Get through, Tish." His wife's name fell from his mouth like an oath. "Get through. I want you to come out back."

"Not now, Duffy. Not today."

"Now," he said.

He went into the kitchen, opened the icebox, and took out a quart bottle filled with a mixture he had made in the blender that morning before he left. It had Hoffman's high-protein and skim milk and bananas and soybeans and raw eggs and honey whipped together with just enough wheat germ to give it a good thick texture. He turned it up and slowly drank it down. Then he went back into the living room, where Tish still had not moved.

"I've already told the boy. He's out back by now."

"Duffy, I don't feel like that stuff this morning."

He kept his voice calm. "It'll only take a few minutes. We won't be but a few minutes."

"Just let me do my thumb," she said.

She looked up at him now and stopped with the tiny lacquer brush poised over her thumb. Her mouth went sour as though she had just tasted something rotten.

"What happened this time?"

"I ran into a wall on the courts."

"Is that blood on your shirt?"

"Yes."

"Look at me."

He looked at her.

"You've knocked a tooth out."

"Yeah, one came out."

"Did you save it? We can put it under your pillow. Maybe the good fairy will bring you some sense."

"Tish, would you get through with that so we can go out back?"

She held the little brush above her thumbnail and did not move.

"You've even broken one. You've broken one in the front of your mouth."

"Tish, if you don't paint that thumb, I think I'll just slap the shit out of you."

"Any day you've got the balls," she said.

It was true he had never hit her, but not because he didn't have the balls for it. He was afraid he would kill her. He was afraid if he ever hit her once, he wouldn't be able to stop.

"You're ugly with that tooth like that," she said. "I want you to go right to the dentist tomorrow and get it fixed so you won't be so ugly."

"I'll go to the dentist. Now don't you think we can do something with the kid, together? He's back there waiting. Maybe you'll get into it this time."

"You go on back. I'll be there as soon as I finish with this thumb."

He would dearly have loved to bite that thumb off, but he only said through clenched teeth: "See if you can make it in less than an hour."

There was a cement terrace almost a hundred feet wide built onto the back of the house. Very old water oaks shaded part of it. Under the shaded part, Duffy placed tatami mats. That was where the boy was sitting now, eating another quarter-pound Baby Ruth. It brought Duffy to the point of despair. But he went on out to where his son was, stripped off his shirt, and sat in the lotus position. Felix couldn't sit in the lotus position. It hurt him. And Tish refused to. She said she was sure it would make her knees ugly.

"How many of those have you had this morning?" asked Duffy.

"This one and the other one."

"Did you have any breakfast?"

"Uh huh."

"What?"

"Krinkles."

"What is Krinkles?"

"Cereal. It comes in chocolate and strawberry. I always get Mom to get the chocolate."

"You like chocolate the best, do you, son?"

"It's got the biggest race car in it," Felix said.

A goddam race car in a goddam box of chocolate cereal. He'd done everything he could think of to try to make the boy human, but none of it had worked.

"Son, do you remember what I told you about eating candy, what it does to your teeth and your body?"

"Uh huh."

"Then why do you keep on eating the stuff?"

He looked up at Duffy with pale blue eyes. The boy held out what was left of the candy bar. "You want me to throw this away?"

Duffy sighed. He had a lot of his mother in him. "It's not that I want you to throw *that* candy bar away, son. I want you to try to understand that that stuff will ruin your body. It's no good."

"You *don't* want me to throw this away?" said the boy.

Duffy felt a quiet madness stealing into his brain. "No, Felix, I don't want you to throw the candy away. Eat it."

The boy peeled back the wrapper and ate it. Duffy thought he never would get through chewing it. Felix made little wet moans of pleasure as his soft cheeks worked over the candy. When he finally did swallow the last bit, he gave Duffy a slow, sad, intimidated smile. He had peanuts and Baby Ruth chocolate and caramel stuck between his teeth.

Duffy loved Felix, he knew he did, but he also knew that he hated what the kid had become. A fucking slug. A huge, soft, white slug. Well, it was still early; he still had time to bring Felix around. He had to. It was necessary for Duffy's own notion of himself. He didn't like to think about it, didn't like to think about it at all, but having such a kid was embarrassing. A father could not have such a son unless the father had failed. The son was the measure of the father. Duffy's own father had taught him that. And even if his father had been a little off center, some even said crazy (suffering from combat psychosis is what they said, but what they *meant* was crazy), look at what the old man had produced in Duffy.

The sliding glass door at the back of the house slammed shut, and Tish came balancing across the terrace on her cork wedges. She was waving her right hand in the air as she came, every step or two pursing her mouth and blowing on her thumb. Duffy watched her moving through the dappled shade, coming slowly, through little pools of sunlight, moving in her own time, totally unconcerned that she had kept him waiting, *was* keeping him waiting. Duffy could not help but admire her, even now. Her legs were long and well-formed, firm thighs pushing up into a tight little ass that moved under her hot pants with a rhythm as controlled as the ticking of a clock. He always admired that, tick-tock, tick-tock, up-down, slip-slide. God, stripped down, she looked so fine.

Duffy watched her coming toward him and wondered where the girl had gone whom he saw all those years ago walking up out of the water at Crescent Beach just south of St. Augustine the day after he had turned twenty-four. He had driven over from Gainesville out of habit, a habit sustained through his undergraduate days at the University of Florida and on through his years there in law school. Crescent Beach was the local meat rack during the warm months, a place where the beautiful young women from the university drifted across the sand, their limbs and various creases lubricated and glistening under a sheen of baby oil. All the while, young men swarmed about them with the mindless and erratic movements of insects around glowing lights.

Totally without thought, like the other men, Duffy had followed her up the beach. She seemed a single extraordinary muscle moving in the sun. He could not believe her hair.

"I uh can't uh believe your hair," he said when he walked up beside her. And then he couldn't believe he'd said what he said. How utterly dumb.

"That's weak," she said, "very feeble."

"I was thinking that too," he said.

"What?"

"Weak. Feeble."

He fell a step behind her as she walked on. Her skin was smooth, without blemish, and the color of milk. There were two dimples in her lower back right above the line of her bikini. He watched the dimples intently until he could feel his heart moving in his chest.

"Hey, why don't we," he said, talking to her back, "pretend you want to meet *me*. That way you can think of something to say, because I can't think of anything that doesn't sound like bullshit." She glanced at him briefly over her shoulder and kept walking. "My name is Duffy Deeter and I'm a lawyer in Gainesville. I came over here to Crescent Beach because I've been doing it forever and because it's Saturday and because

I'm severely bored." She walked on. "I really was struck by your hair. It's beautiful but more than that, it's uh, well, *weird.*"

This time when she glanced over her shoulder she smiled. "Where's Gainesville?"

A week later, the following Saturday night, lying in his bed with sweat running between her breasts, she told him she had decided to talk to him when he said her hair was weird. He didn't answer but watched the triangle of silver where it glowed between her legs.

"Nobody ever said anything like that about my hair," she said.

"I probably wouldn't have either, but I couldn't think of anything else."

She said: "There's worse things than being thrown back upon the truth."

"You want the truth, lady? I'll give you the truth. You fuck like Genghis Khan went to war. *That* is the truth."

A savage little smile came on her mouth. "I don't want to throw you *back* on it. I want you on top of it, under it, behind it, in it. I . . . I . . ."

She came at him again. And it was like fucking a squirrel. She went up one side of him and down the other. What wings they had in those days, how they could fly!

Duffy watched her in her hot pants there on the patio and struggled to remember when she had become a walking sexual disaster. He couldn't take her around the bend anymore, had not been able to for a very long time. She didn't seem to want to go anymore, and he could not bring himself to ask her why. But whatever the reason, Duffy would just as soon hump a pound of cold calves' liver as what Tish had become. Rather, in fact, because at least liver wouldn't say, every fourth stroke: *You about through?* stroke stroke stroke stroke *You about through?* And Tish would never lie any quieter in her coffin than she lay in bed.

"Well, have you boys been having a nice talk out here?" she asked in her bright, careless voice.

"Uh huh," Felix grunted, showing her his candied teeth.

Tish sat down. "Well, here we are," she said.

5   "Remember," said Duffy, settling deeper into his
lotus position, "the strength of Zen is that it has nothing to
teach."

"Ah, Duff, do we have to go through this again?" she asked.

"Yes," he said, "because you have not learned it."

"Of course we've learned it. Haven't we, Felix? Don't you
remember Daddy saying that?"

"Uh huh," said Felix, sucking his teeth,

"I know you remember it. Now I want you to learn it."

"Ah, Duff," said Tish.

"Ah, Dad," said Felix.

"Zen is not teaching," said Duffy. "It is vision. It is accept-
ance. Remember, we are now thinking of the One, a balance of
nature—both the human and the not-human, a universal vision
of life as the Tao or way of nature in which the good and the
evil, the creative and the destructive, the wise and the foolish,
are the inseparable polarities of existence. Remember, Tao is
that from which one cannot depart. That from which one can
depart is not the Tao."

"Jesus Christ," sighed Tish.

Duffy had his eyes partially shut, letting only a little light
sift through the lashes, trying to concentrate on what he was

saying, as much for himself as for them. Because even as he spoke, he felt the bicycle ticking in his hot calves, the girl's teeth pressing against his heavy shoulders, and behind his half-closed eyes the images of death flickered relentlessly. That was what had brought him to Zen to start with, an effort to find a counterpoint to his own compulsion to compete with himself, a compulsion that turned every craft and skill into a marathon of self-discipline.

But he couldn't explain to them what Zen was, much less why he was doing it, why he knew that Zen was the other side of himself.

"Jesus Christ," sighed Tish again.

"We'll do a few koans and then quit," said Duffy.

"Good. All right," Tish said.

Duffy looked at her with loving hatred and said: "When your spirit is high, augment your spirit. Where there is no style there is also some style."

Her brows drew together, shattering her brittle alabaster face. "Where there is no style there is also some style?" she demanded.

"Right," said Duffy, happy in his heart. "Now one that has a nice story with it."

"And we have to hear the story, right?" said Tish.

"Cho and Hu," said Duffy, "were two men of ancient China, famous for their integrity. When the emperor Ya, who incidentally lived two thousand three hundred and fifty-seven years before the Jesus Christ you keep mumbling about, when Ya offered his throne to Hu, the old man hurried to wash his ears in a stream, in order to clean them. Cho, hearing of this, led his ox upstream to drink so that it would not be dirtied by water in which Hu had washed his ears. It is out of this story that we have one of the most famous koans."

A silence stretched after his words. The noon woods ticked around them. Felix sucked his teeth.

"Which is?" said Tish.

Duffy said: "Cho waters his ox, Hu washes his ears."

Her face, which had been clearly showing her irritation, went suddenly blank, almost stunned.

"Cho waters his ox?" she said. "Hu washes his ears?"

"That's it," said Duffy. "Cho waters his ox, Hu washes his ears. You've got to think about it. Meditate on it. Somewhere in there is the heart of all knowledge."

"Duffy Deeter," she said in a quiet deadly voice. She was standing now, glaring down upon him from above, those beautiful legs straddling that worthless pad of white hair. "You kept me out here, telling me that story, wasting my time? Cho waters his goddam ox, and Hu washes his fucking ears?"

Duffy was smiling. The whole inside of his chest was lifting. "I didn't make it up," he said. "It's older than Rome. It was ancient when they took the pins out of Christ on the cross."

Her face was flushed and she seemed to be trembling. But she could not speak. She turned and marched stiffly back into the house. Duffy watched her go, thinking if she could only manage to get a little of that kind of passion in her blood when she was in bed, she probably wouldn't be such a lousy lay.

"Can I go now?"

Duffy turned and the boy was smiling shyly and sadly at him. Felix had cleaned his teeth up pretty well, but the little triangular open spaces in his gums were still packed with refined sugar and chocolate and stale peanuts and caramel sludge.

"No, son, you can't," said Duffy Deeter.

"I can't?" said the boy.

"Nope," Duffy said.

"You going to tell me some more of them things? About washing the ox's ears?"

"The man washing his ears," said Duffy. "The ox only drank the water."

"You going to tell some more?"

"No," said Duffy. "Nothing like that. You're going to come up to the weightroom and have a little workout with me."

"*I'm* going to work out?" said the boy.

"That's right."

"With the weights?"

"Yes."

"Like you do?"

"Yes."

"Why?"

Duffy wanted to say: *Because you have Baby Ruth in your teeth.* But he didn't. The boy had been up to the weightroom and seen his father pumping iron. And Duffy knew the boy was terrified of the place—the sweat, the grunts, the sudden explosions of breath.

"It comes to every man, son," said Duffy.

"What does?" Felix asked.

"The time, son. The time comes. Let's go."

Felix got awkwardly to his feet and followed Duffy around the house and up a curving set of iron steps to the room built above the garage. The four walls, ceiling and floor were all done in cypress. It was air-conditioned, and windowless. A bar was built at one end of the room. It, too, was made of cypress and the top of it was covered with bowls of apples and oranges and carrots and pears and mangoes and garlic. (Duffy Deeter was a constant and voracious eater of garlic because he was convinced it was one of the great strength foods of the world.) In the middle of the bar was a two-and-a-half-foot-tall blender, a machine designed to turn anything that was put into it into juice.

Dominating the room, sitting squarely in the middle of it, was the Universal, about eight feet long and four feet wide, a machine made of pulleys and steel plates and chrome bars. Any muscle in the body could be isolated on it and worked to exhaustion.

Duffy slipped out of his shoes. He always liked to work out barefoot. He turned to his son, who had not come into the room but had stopped in the doorway and was now staring balefully at his father with his pale washed-blue eyes.

"Close the door and strip out of your shirt, son," said Duffy. "Take your pants off too."

The child actually blushed, which made Duffy want to hit him.

"My pants?"

Duffy said: "You can't work out in those tight clothes."

Felix was always breathlessly constricted by the belt that cut his fat little belly, and his bulging thighs were creased and straining, and his fat cheeks were always chewing hungrily at his trousers.

The boy still had not moved. "I'll have to go downstairs and get my swim trunks," he said.

"Your drawers'll do fine," Duffy said. "Now close the door and strip down."

Duffy knew if he let the kid out of the room, he'd go straight to his mother. She had forbidden Duffy to ever let Felix touch the Universal. She said it would make him a hard and lumpy child, and that having a hard and lumpy husband was already bad enough. They had argued about it endlessly since the boy had started snoring just after his third birthday.

"He wouldn't snore if he was working out. It'll help his breathing," Duffy had told her, "jogging, pumping a little iron, stuff like that."

"He's only a baby, Duffy."

"He snores and he's overweight. I've got to get him on a program."

"Don't you dare."

"Then you do it, goddammit. I don't care just as long as he's got one."

It was no accident that she had looked like a single shimmering muscle that day when he met her on Crescent Beach. She was an extraordinary athlete, a gymnast, and it had been while watching her work out on the uneven bars that he first had the notion that he loved her, that he wanted to marry her. Wasn't it just as easy to fall in love with a good gene pool as a bad one? Of course it was. And being an athlete herself, she would pass along to his children her enthusiasm for sweat and pain. But it had not worked out that way. Even though she maintained a schedule for herself of aerobics, dance and work-outs on the balance beam, she treated Felix like a delicate, exotic pet. It drove Duffy into a fury if he let himself think about it. And today he was thinking about it.

Felix was finally down to his shorts, and Duffy, who had seen him practically every day of his life galumphing around the house naked, looked at him now the way he always looked at him. It was exactly the way Jert looked at his belly. Amazement and disbelief. Felix was made entirely of curves. There was not a straight line or a right angle on his body. And the flesh seemed to have no substance, as though there might not be any bones in him. The boy walked over to the Universal machine, his deeply naveled belly jiggling as he walked and his ass eating vigorously at his Jockey shorts.

"How much do I have to do?" Felix asked.

"All of it, son," said Duffy. "You have to do it all."

They stood regarding the machine.

"It seems like a lot," said Felix.

"It is a lot," Duffy said. "I'll just run through this quickly so you'll get some idea of what you're going to do." He stared at his son, who was digging in his mouth with his finger. Duffy pointed at the various seats and benches built around the four sides of the Universal. "Son, these are the fourteen stations of man. As a matter of fact, there *is* a man in that machine. Look at it! Stare at it, Felix! He's in there. Buried in those cables and steel plates and benches and pulleys and bars is a man. He is looking at you. Look back at him, boy! Stare him dead in the eye. He is whoever you want him to be. He's got the kind of chest you want him to have, the kind of arms, the kind of legs. That man is in there, buried in that metal, and he wants to come out! He wants to come out and be you!" He paused, then: "On your back, Felix. On your back, boy." Felix fell fatly onto the bench. Duffy adjusted the cables to fifteen pounds.

"Pump it twelve times!"

Felix pumped.

"Breathe! Breathe!" Duffy shouted so loud that a single enormous tear appeared on Felix's trembling cheek. Duffy pretended not to see it. When Felix was finished, Duffy adjusted the cables again, going this time to three hundred. While he pumped he talked. "We'll keep it light for you." Pump, pump. "But high reps." Pump, pump. "Go through every station." Pump, pump. "Three sets." Pump, pump. "You'll be sore as hell tomorrow." Pump. "But that's . . ." Puuummmppp. ". . . the price."

With infinite sadness, Felix flopped onto the bench when his father got up. Duffy adjusted the weight and Felix was off again, with Duffy shouting: "Breathe! Breathe!" After three sets on the prone press, they went to the lat machine and from there to the overhead presses and then to upright rowing and on and on, around the machine. Felix's skin was getting pinker and pinker and his eyes more and more dazed. Duffy was in a frenzy. He kept thinking: Hell, this is me I'm working, my flesh and my bone and my blood. He's a little me. I'm in him. And by goddam I will come out.

Duffy made it last one hour exactly. Then he led his trembling son over to the bar, threw fifteen carrots, two mangoes, five oranges, two apples and six huge lumps of garlic into his juicer, flipped a switch, and almost instantly removed a tall glass of thick, slightly green fluid, and said: "Take a big hit off this, Felix. You did fine, just fine. A big hit of this'll bring you back."

The boy's glazed eyes never even turned on the glass when it was put in his hand. He mechanically raised it to his swollen, panting mouth and drank. Then he shot a spray of vomit all over Duffy.

"*What in God's name . . . in God's name . . .*"

Duffy turned to see Tish, rigid and screaming, in the doorway. The vomit was a mixture of slightly green juice and undigested, poorly chewed Baby Ruth candy. It smelled as though it had come from the stomach of a camel.

"You insane bastard, you've ruined Felix."

Felix staggered over to his mother, where he stood panting. Duffy stripped off his shirt and dropped it to the floor.

"He only threw up, Tish. It's not the end of the world."

"You'll . . . you'll by God think it is," Tish screamed. One of her hands was buried in her carefully arranged hair as though she meant to tear it out by the roots.

"Does this mean you're not coming in the Winnebago?"

"What do you think?"

"Actually, I've thought for a while that you didn't mean to come with me."

"What I mean to do is see a lawyer. You sonofabitch, six weeks from now you won't own a Winnebago or anything else. Look what you've done to Felix! What *have* you done to him?"

Duffy regarded his son, whose pink tongue beat like a pulse between his parted lips.

"Changed him a little, I hope," Duffy said.

"You've finally gone over the edge," said Tish. Her hand had come out of her hair and her voice was calm now, distant, icy. "You have, finally."

"How about you, Felix? You want to come with me?"

The boy drew closer to his mother and did not speak.

"There," said Tish with some satisfaction. "Is that answer enough for you?"

For a long moment, Felix watched Duffy with unsure eyes before his mother took him by the hand and led him out of the workout room. After they were gone, Duffy said quietly: "Yeah, that's answer enough."

It was late afternoon before Duffy left in the Winnebago. He was laughing when he started up the drive, but before he got to the street a great wave of senseless anguish broke upon him and changed the laughter to something else. Anybody hearing him as he drove through the darkening streets would not have known whether the sound he was making was one of joy or despair. Duffy did not know himself. And in that moment, what he knew of the world made it not matter at all, made it seem, in fact, precisely right.

6

Duffy stood on the track with a stopwatch in his hand. It was an old cinder track behind a run-down country school. Some black kids were shooting basketball on a cement court and their voices drifted to him across the packed dirt of the playground, streaked red with the last rays of the sun.

The day was cooler now and Duffy felt strong as he bent to stretch his hamstrings. It was a quarter-mile track and he had already run two slow laps to warm up. It was time to do it. No more bullshit now. He glanced again at the stopwatch. He wanted a four-thirty mile and he was not sure he could do it. But he would know pretty soon. And that was the point, to have an answer, an unarguable answer. He set himself to start, and as he came off the line with the first long driving stride, his thumb hit the button to start the watch. As he made the turn nearest the basketball court, the kids stopped to watch him.

"Hey! That ole sucker can fly!"

"He be running some, Jack!"

Their high excited voices made Duffy feel good. He concentrated on relaxing and holding his form. He was glad to be running. Whatever happened later would take care of itself. But this was the right thing to be doing now.

After Duffy left his house, he bellowed, laughed and howled

for the better part of half an hour, by which time he was out of
town on Highway 20, without the slightest notion of where he
was going. Or if in fact he wanted to go anywhere at all. But
wanting had nothing to do with it. He had to go *somewhere*. On
the dash of the Winnebago was a packet of reservations: a hotel
in Miami, airline tickets to Kingston, Jamaica, more hotel reservations. But that was all off now. Just as well. He didn't know
how he would have survived two weeks of more or less constant
companionship with a family that had been for a long time now
festering like a sore for which there was no remedy. Well, he
didn't have to worry about the vacation now. That bridge was
burned.

He drove mindlessly on, but he was increasingly aware
something was wrong. He was going down. Something was leak-
ing out of him like a bad tire going flat. He tried to think what
it was. It couldn't be the thing with Tish. That had been coming
for so long he was only relieved that it was over. But of course
he could not be sure it was over! They'd had fights before. Maybe
this was just one more in a long series that would go on forever.
He thought he missed his son, but he was honest enough with
himself to admit he didn't know. The child revolted him, at least
at times. Could you love someone who constantly revolted you?
The answer to that was easy: certainly. Revulsion seemed to be
a necessary part of love. The thought made him feel somewhat
better. It would all just have to work itself out.

He was passing the little town of Hawthorne, when he suddenly cried: "Kick ass and take names! Goddammit, son, *do* it!
Fall'm in, feed'm beans, and stamp'm duty, Sarge!"

But his voice came into his ears hollow and defeated. Jesus,
he had to get control of this, get on top of whatever this feeling
was. His head had somehow gone wrong, taken a bad turn. It
wouldn't do to excuse himself simply because he had woken up
that morning thinking about the strange turn of events that had
lost him the whiplash case, and then had that followed by an
unrelievedly terrible day. And the thought that maybe it had

42

been an unrelievedly good day too, but that he was not human enough to recognize it, did not help.

Just as he was thinking that this endless speculation would not do, he saw a pair of bent goalposts through his side window and beyond the goalposts a ragged practice field and beyond that a quarter-mile cinder track. He swung the Winnebago to the side of the road and before he had even stopped it he was reaching behind the seat for his Nike training bag, which held his flat-soled middle-distance shoes, running briefs and singlet, and finally his stopwatch.

The stopwatch. He felt better the moment he touched it. For him it was a kind of metaphor that contained everything clean, lucid and ultimately understandable. That was why he loved sports. Sports were made up of a system of measures that never lied. If a man said he could prone press 450 pounds, you could put him on a bench. He either could do it or he could not. And if somebody claimed to have four-four speed in the forty-yard dash, you could put a watch on him. You could not bullshit a stopwatch.

But you could bullshit everything else. Everything. The image of Tish's father floated up out of the cinder track and he considered it in a kind of abstracted way to keep his mind off the four-thirty pace which was starting to burn his lungs. Edward "Hands" Martin was a fat but solid man with a florid, smiling face and a manner that was wildly exuberant, bordering at times— it seemed to Duffy—on hysteria.

"Hands!" he screamed at Duffy when Tish introduced them shortly after he met her on Crescent Beach. "Just call me *Hands!*"

"It's a pleasure to meet you, Mr. Martin," Duffy said. "I was saying to Tish—"

"I said *Hands!*" cried Tish's father. He spread his hands out for Duffy to inspect. "Look at those babies!"

They *were* enormous hands, dusted across the back with freckles and sprouting thick red hairs, and Duffy was trying to think of something to say about them, but as it turned out he didn't have to say anything because they were standing in the

43

condominium the Martin family kept on St. Augustine Beach for vacations and Hands suddenly spun around and looked through the wide glass window at the beach, where children played in the surf. "Water!" he shouted. "Will you look at that! The ocean. It lifts your spirits when nothing else can. What do you think?"

What Duffy thought was that he should never have come here to meet this man, that he ought to be back in Gainesville, laid up on his water bed driving Tish like a truck. Hands was carefully coiffed, color-coordinated in a polyester leisure suit, complete with white belt and white shoes, just the sort of costume that lawyers affected and that Duffy hated. There was no help for it, though. Hands was Tish's father and Duffy had to meet him. But he didn't have to like him.

"It's very nice, uh, Hands," said Duffy.

Hands spun around, his voice dropping dead serious. "It's better than that. It's life. And life's my game."

He whipped out a small business card and handed it to Duffy. Duffy glanced at it. EDWARD "HANDS" MARTIN'S GLAD TO SEE YOUR BACK. Underneath it was the curving picture of a spine. When Duffy looked up, Tish's father was again holding out his palms for inspection.

"There's life in those hands. Heal the sick. Make the lame walk. You want to talk arthritis, bursitis, fallen arches, earaches, toothaches, aches of the lumbar region, dizziness and nausea? It's all in the spine. Have you had your spine manipulated?"

"Yes, sir, I have," Duffy said. He was lying, but he thought it was cheap at the price if he could avoid having Mr. Martin throw him to the floor and manipulate his spine, which seemed a distinct possibility.

"Good," said Hands. "It shows you are a sensible man. I like a sensible man."

After saying that, they had cocktails on the terrace—cocktails made from carrot juice and sweet rum. Remarkable. And while they sipped the drinks Hands told Duffy about Tish's mother, who had stayed in Connecticut because she couldn't get away from her school, a school of her own design in which "the entire curriculum was suppleness."

"You would not believe what that woman can do," Hands said, freshening their drinks from a pitcher he brought from the kitchen. "Forty-eight years old and she can still put her feet behind her head, *both* feet behind her head."

Duffy watched Tish and wondered if she could put both of her feet behind *her* head. Tish only smiled and nodded in a fetching way as her father talked about bones over dinner, even as Duffy noticed that each piece of silverware was engraved with the image of a spine.

"The spine has been my life," said Hands. "Amazing device. The centerpiece of the whole body, fitted together out of strangely shaped, flat bones called vertebrae, each vertebra separated by cushions called discs. You know what it is, Duffy, the spine?"

Duffy said, "No, sir, I don't."

"It is the Buddha out of which all goodness and mercy flows because it tightly embraces the core of us all, the vital central cord of life."

"Extraordinary," said Duffy.

"Extraordinary, indeed. But not the half of it. Let me fill you in."

Hands filled him in on the fact that Duffy probably had 206 bones. Although he might have as many as 209. Healthy people sometimes had an extra rib. Maybe even two. Near the neck. He could also have an extra bone or two in his coccyx. Did Duffy know that his entire skeleton would weigh no more than twenty pounds, but that his shinbone alone could hold up an automobile containing four passengers? Duffy did not know that. True though. It was because bone was so flexible, twenty times more resilient than steel. If it were more like metal, it would break much more easily than it did. But fortunately it was not at all like metal.

"We can be grateful for that if nothing else," said Duffy.

"Certainly can," said Hands, not even blinking at Duffy's sarcasm. "Certainly can."

Hands carved himself another dripping slice of meat from

45

the leg of lamb and Duffy wondered if he knew that every five pounds of fat on his stomach put an additional fifty pounds of pressure on his back, on the spine he was so fond of talking about. But of course he knew. It was hardly a secret why pregnant women had backaches. It was just Hands' bullshit, bullshit for himself and for anybody else who would buy it. Knowing had nothing to do with it.

Knowing, like thinking, accomplished nothing. That certainty gave enormous comfort and a surge of strength to Duffy as he held the pace around the track, the black kids on the basketball court shouting and urging him on each time he passed them. No, he had no faith in thinking. Thinking always left you precisely where you were. You couldn't think your way out of a gas chamber or across barbed wire. The act was the thing.

"The act is the thing," he had gasped, his mouth pressed against Tish's ear, later that night.

"Oh, yes, oooohhhh, God, yes," sang Tish there on her back where he rode her under the dark castle wall.

"No, no, not that," he said, without breaking the rhythm of the ride. "You don't understand. But you will. I'll make you understand."

"Make me. Yes. Make me, you darling."

After they had left her father, he had walked with Tish down St. Augustine Beach, to the enormous Spanish fort, Castillo de San Marcos, where he had lain with her in the dark grass with the surf pounding behind them, and he had found out that yes, she *could* put both her feet behind her head.

"Osceola," he said, breathing hard, "Osceola, great chief of the Seminole, put his knife through a treaty of surrender. An act, *the* act."

"Yes," Tish said. "God, yes, the act is the thing."

His grunting breath coming counterpoint to his words, he said, "Osceola told them his knife was his answer to their treaty of surrender."

"Surrender," she said, her voice distant, lost now, he knew, to the moment and to him. "Surrender."

46

"They did finally take him, though, under a flag of truce and shut him up here in this fort forever. But he always had the memory of his knife."

"His knife," she said.

"His knife," he said, "the moment, the *act*."

He rounded the curve by the basketball court and was on the last hundred-yard straight of the mile. The kids were on the edge of the track, shouting to him.

"Fly, man, *fly!*" one of them cried.

"Drive, drive, run on *through* it!"

"Pump, pump, lift, lift it *all!*"

Full into his kick as he passed them, Duffy concentrated on keeping his head still, holding his form, full out all the way. He touched the button on the stopwatch as he flew across the finish line. He jogged another two hundred yards before he started walking back toward the Winnebago. He had cooled out, his breathing back to normal, before he looked at his stopwatch. He hadn't turned the four-thirty. He was only eleven seconds short of a full five minutes. But he was neither surprised nor disappointed. It was a good solid answer to a good solid question and it was enough. After all, it had been a long day. He'd had nothing at the end, no kick at all. A four-forty-nine mile was not a bad time, certainly not a bad time for a man his age. It simply was not the time he wanted, the time he knew he was capable of turning. He would have to go back to interval training and to more sprint work.

By the time he opened the door and stepped up into the Winnebago, he was feeling better than he had all day. He replaced the watch in his Nike training bag, stripped out of his shorts and singlet, and threw them into a hamper. On the way to the shower he paused in the short passageway joining the driver's compartment to the master bedroom. On both walls of the passageway were long shelves of books locked in behind a metal grate so they could not slide out at sudden stops and turns. He didn't like to be too far from his books. They were—the best of them, anyway—efforts to get a handle on the world, to name the abyss, to wrestle with it, and at the same time to avoid bullshit.

His eye fell on a three-foot shelf of poetry, and finally stopped on a title by Leonard Cohen: *Flowers for Hitler.* He could remember that there was a poem in it called "Goebbels Abandons His Novel and Joins the Party." He had read and reread the book many times, but try as he would, he could remember none of it. He thought that normally he could remember it. He had read Leonard Cohen's novel, *Beautiful Losers,* also. But he could remember nothing about it except the title. He stood staring at the book of poetry. What was a Jew doing writing something with Hitler in the title? Particularly *flowers* for Hitler. Maybe it was because Leonard Cohen was a loser. A beautiful loser. Maybe it was because losers are winners. Consider the fact that one great writer's work often stood diametrically opposed in style and content to another great writer's work. Strange, very strange. But Hitler *was* dead. And the last time he had heard of Leonard Cohen, he was singing on the radio.

On the shelf below the poetry, he searched for a novel to read on Crescent Beach tonight, because he had decided out on the track that Crescent Beach was where he was going to stay until the morning, when he would return to Gainesville and get enough money out of the bank to take him as far away as he needed to go from his law practice and Jert, from his wife and Marvella, enough money to stay as long as he needed to stay. He opened the grate and took out one of his favorite books, Graham Greene's *The Power and the Glory.* He knew it was the book he needed because the moment he saw it, he remembered the whole thing as vividly as he remembered his own father, dead now these many years. He remembered the man at the center of the book, a wonderful, totally fucked-up priest, a Catholic priest who is a drunk, who has a child out of wedlock, and who is at the same time God's man in the world. The priest does not just believe he is God's man, or just know he is God's man, but he *acts* on the knowledge and belief to administer last rites even though in his time and place Catholicism has been out-lawed. And the penalty for administering last rites is death. Totally flawed and fucked up, the priest remains the perfect instrument of God. Wonderful. Everything works together. Everything is of a piece. The thing to do is to be able to recognize it. Today was rage and outrage.

Duffy had had such days before, enough of them so they were no longer a surprise. That's why he kept part of his collection of taped speeches in the Winnebago. He never liked to be too far away from his speeches. Great speeches of the world. Great speeches by not necessarily great men. He had a memorable organizing speech by the Grand Wizard of the Ku Klux Klan and he had Martin Luther King speaking at the Lincoln Memorial in Washington, D.C. He had Winston Churchill after Dunkirk and Roosevelt after Pearl Harbor. And of course he had Hitler.

After he had showered and changed into fresh clothes, he slipped Der Führer into his sound system and set the volume high. With what sounded like all the Germans in the world Sieg Heiling their asses off, he leapt back into the seat and roared off toward Crescent Beach.

It was dark when he pulled down on the beach and parked. A full moon hung over the Atlantic. A yellow path of light ran toward him across the water and stopped right outside the window of the Winnebago. He thought a night beside the ocean would help him. The gently lapping waves, the rushing wind, would be soothing, would help him sort things out, although he was not sure what precisely needed sorting out or if it was at all sortable.

He poured himself a whiskey and sat in a chair under a little yellow light, reading *The Power and the Glory*. The whiskey was warm in his stomach and he had read the novel so many times it was like a conversation with an old friend. It could be picked up anywhere, begun anywhere, and so he watched the priest carry the holy book around under a pornographic cover and get drunk on the sacramental wine and tend to the souls of men in the steaming jungles of Mexico where religion had been out-lawed at about the time when Duffy was born. Eventually, his eyes became tired, and he put the book aside and turned out the light. Slowly, so as not to disturb the tenuous peace he had found with himself, he slipped out of his clothes and lay naked on the bed. He closed his eyes and forced himself to breathe regularly. He prided himself on being a good sleeper. But sleep did not come. The uneasy peace melted from him and he felt the muscles of his neck and shoulders becoming strangely tense. Finally, he opened his eyes. Something was wrong. What the hell was it? He sighed, rose from the bed, and went outside to stand on the beach.

Just to the north shone the lights of St. Augustine. The huge monolith of the Castillo de San Marcos stood darker against the darkening sky, and he could see, or thought he could, the building where Tish's family had kept their condominium. Hands Martin was gone now, dead of a heart attack. And Tish's mother, that dear lady who could put both her feet behind her head right up to the time she broke her neck skiing in Aspen, was gone as well. The sweet girl Duffy had told the story of Osceola, that passionate, panting, delightfully sweaty girl, was gone too. The woman he had left back in Gainesville screaming about their ruined son bore no resemblance to the girl he had lain with under the dark wall of the Castillo de San Marcos all those years ago.

He thought again of Hands, could hear him over the wash of the surf.

"His name is Jesus," Hands would say, "the one true friend. Call him anytime. His number is John three:sixteen."

Hands had a thing about thanking Jesus. It was bigger than his thing with bones. It turned out that Hands thanked Jesus more or less constantly. A red light would turn green and Hands, sitting in his huge Cadillac, would say, "Thank you, Jesus." Anything and everything was enough to set him to thanking Jesus. But Duffy knew it was bullshit, knew that in his secret heart, Hands was always saying, "And thank you, Jesus, if you could just see fit to jerk a few lower backs out of whack and send them

50

to a Hands Haven of Chiropractic Medicine, I'd appreciate it, and thank you, Jesus." Hands had had chiropractic clinics all across the country even when he himself no longer practiced. Duffy sighed. Hands hadn't been a bad guy, just full of shit.

Duffy watched the moon and the path of yellow light pouring toward him across the water. He listened carefully to the hissing break of waves and the rushing wind. And then he knew what it was, the reason he couldn't sleep. The sound was wrong. Bad and artificial. It was as though the ocean and the wind had been recorded in an inferior studio and played back through a flawed system. Warped turntable. Cheap amplifiers. He went back into the camper and closed all the windows and selected one of his high-performance cassettes. On the label across the front of the tape was the legend *Ocean and Wind*. He put it on, turned the sound up, and got back into bed. There. That was it. He was immediately soothed and rocked by the sound of the sea, the primordial, eternal sea, played through the best system money could buy—that is, consistent with the limitations of space imposed by his modified Winnebago. He drifted into a deep sleep and did not dream.

The next morning he awoke early, as was his habit, and watched the sun lift out of the ocean. To knock off the rough edges of frustration and anxiety from the day before, he decided to work out. In nothing but a jockstrap, he climbed the ladder to the gym he had built directly above the master bedroom. The ceiling of the gym was too low to do standing presses, but he had a good bench from which he could do prone presses, inclined presses, pull-overs, leg extensions for quadriceps muscles above the knees, and many ingenious exercises to brutalize and terrorize all the provinces of his body. Louvered windows on either side of the low room brought him the false sound of the wind and sea while he worked.

By the time he had finished his workout, which included a slow three-mile jog, and had driven back to Gainesville, it was early afternoon. He walked into the bank only twenty minutes before it closed. He wrote out a check for fifteen hundred dollars and went to a teller, a pleasant young woman whom he had known for a long time.

"Good morning, Mr. Deeter," she said, giving him a bright smile which he recognized instantly as strained and artificial.

Remembering the way the water and wind had sounded the night before, he thought: Jesus, is everything going to seem phony? But he said: "Good afternoon, Ruth. How be thee this fine spring day?"

"Fine. And how be thee?"

The how-be-thee exchange was a thing they'd been doing for years, and it had always seemed right and good-natured. But today it only seemed wrong and silly. Ruth took the check from him and turned it in her hands, looking at it as though she had never seen one before. Duffy realized with a start that she was blushing.

"Is there something wrong?" he asked.

She put the check back on the counter in front of her, equidistant between them, and did not look at him when she spoke. "I'm afraid Mrs. Deeter was already in this morning."

Duffy simply stared back at her. Afraid? Afraid she was in? "I don't under . . ." And then he understood. Lines from an old Hank Williams song played in his head. *When I went down to the bank this morning, teller met me with a grin. Said I'm so sorry for you, Hank, but your wife's done been in.* "You mean she took it all? Closed the account?"

"No," said the teller, still not looking at him.

"Good," said Duffy.

"She left two dollars and eight cents."

"Oh," said Duffy. "What about the savings? . . ."

"She left two dollars and eight cents in that too."

"Well," said Duffy. "Well."

"I guess so," said the teller.

Duffy took the check off the counter and carefully tore it in half. He felt a savage, joyous enthusiasm rising in him. He'd found another wall, another barrier, another challenge. His heart sang. Who could tell where this would end?

52

As he was turning to leave, he winked at the teller. "In this greatest of the world's democracies, it happens every day in the best of families."

"Uh, Mr. Deeter?" Duffy turned back to her. "Uh, Mr. McPhester was with your, uh, wife and he said if you should come in . . . uh, that he'd like you to stop by the office for a minute."

Duffy's grin grew more maniacal. "Thank you," he said over his shoulder, already heading for the door on his ball-bearing stride.

Jert with Tish. More and more interesting. Something to focus on. War. This was probably open war, all the stops pulled. In his Winnebago again, Duffy sped through the heat-distorted streets of Gainesville, whipping around corners, twice narrowly missing university students, the top-heavy camper rocking dangerously.

7   The law offices of Deeter and McPhester were on the second floor of a glass and brick building of modern design, brutal and inhuman, or so Duffy thought. He took the stairs three at a time. The secretary looked up as he burst through the door. Her face flushed and she turned to look out the window. My, my, Duffy thought, all these blushes and averted eyes. But he knew he did in fact have an embarrassing social disease, the rampant disease of the disintegrating family. Well, he told himself as he headed for his office, everything disintegrates and from the disintegration something else is born, a natural law like gravity.

He let himself into his office, which was as bare and austere as a monk's cell. His desk was plain, natural wood, the three chairs ladder-backed and straight, the floor naked. His law degree was the only thing hanging on the wall behind his desk. The way he furnished his office had always infuriated Jert McPhester, who kept insisting that they had an image to keep up. Jert's office looked like the harem of an Arab sheik: an ankle-deep pile carpet on the floor, paintings of the most garish design on the wall, gold pen holders on a carved mahogany desk. Twentieth Century Tacky was what it was, Duffy thought.

But it wasn't Jert's fault. Jert's problem was that he could never forgive himself for having come out of the headwaters of the Suwannee River where it rose in the Okefenokee Swamp. He was a genuine redneck who had been raised in a house that had wooden windows and a tin roof, a huge slow-talking grit who had played his high school ball in Waycross, Georgia, and then been recruited by every big college in the country. After he had made All-America and had sacrificed his knee for the University of Florida, a grateful fag alumnus had seen to it that Jert had financial backing to go to law school. But there were not enough football honors or degrees in the world to make Jert forgive himself for being raised in a pinewoods shack on catfish, gator tail and swamp cabbage. That was why he tricked himself out in clothes only a pimp could admire and decorated his office to look like a high-priced whorehouse.

Jert thought Duffy furnished his office so plainly because he was so stingy, just as Tish no doubt thought—if she thought anything—that he objected to the fourth couch because it was a waste of money. Wasting money had nothing to do with it. Duffy never hesitated to spend money on anything that had a function. The elaborately modified Winnebago was necessary. The collection of tapes, the speaker system, the books, the gymnasium in the top, and ultimately the mobility of the Winnebago all collaborated to keep Duffy sane. But four couches were unreasonable and had no function. The same was true of the stuff Jert surrounded himself with, everything from the way he decorated his office to the car he drove.

A small, ugly iron safe sat in one corner of Duffy's office. He went to it and worked the combination. When the heavy door swung back, Duffy took out a velvet sack big as a cantaloupe. It was filled with gold Krugerrands, thick gold coins from the mines of South Africa. Cover your six, his daddy used to say. His daddy had been a fighter pilot and six o'clock is always directly behind the pilot. Cover your six—cover your ass—because if you don't, nobody else will. Duffy had tried to do that, cover his ass. That was the reason for the Krugerrands in his office safe rather than in a safe-deposit box in a bank. He wanted his gold where he could put his hands on it.

He had taken half the coins from the velvet bag and closed the safe when Jert came in, his belly swinging under the vest of his three-piece polyester color-coordinated suit.

"Hey, Duffy," said Jert. "I was hoping you might drop by today. I—"

"The teller at the bank told me," said Duffy, giving Jert his most vicious smile.

"Then you know that—"

"I know the bitch cleaned me out at the bank."

Jert's face was pained, serious. "Ah, Duffy, don't call that sweet lady a bitch. These things are always difficult."

Duffy wondered if Jert had been pumping Tish. If he had, it would not surprise Duffy, but then nothing human surprised him. Tish had the rankest kind of taste in everything. Fat, larcenous Jert was just the sort of man she would admire. And Duffy figured a pound of cold calves' liver would be about all Jert could handle every night between the sheets. Duffy told himself that he did not care, that he even hoped it was true. They deserved each other.

"What things, Jert? What's always difficult?"

Jert took a deep breath and barked the word like a football signal: "Divorce."

Duffy said: "You know entirely too much about my life. You're pretty thick with Tish, Coach."

"I'm representing her," said Jert.

"Representing her in what?"

"In everything."

Duffy could feel the vein leap in his forehead. He started for the door. Jert glided into his path as smoothly as a ballet dancer. He still had great balance for a ruined jock who was running to fat. "Where you going, Duff?"

"I thought I'd go over and see if I could make Tish eat the money she took out of our joint accounts."

Jert did not move out of his way. "I wouldn't do that, Duff."

"There's very little I do that you'd do. Or could do."

"Please don't make this more difficult than it is."

"Jert, you're going to make me throw up."

"You can't go over there anymore."

Duffy's hands rose as if of their own will, rigid and flat as boards, formed to strike with the oxbone just above the wrist.

Still Jert did not move. And Duffy considered the fact that Jert *had* speared some of the most dangerous and bad-assed running backs in the Southeastern Conference in his day.

Jert sighed. "She's got a restraining order, Duff. If you go to that house, you'll be in jail in twenty minutes. You are expressly forbidden to go to the house or speak to her. We have attached all assets whatsoever pending the outcome of the divorce proceedings."

"You should have stayed out of this, Jert."

"She needed counsel. She came to me. You wouldn't have expected me to turn her away, would you? You know I've only got her best interests at heart. Hers and yours."

"I've got her best interests swinging," said Duffy.

"This belligerence is going to get you in serious trouble someday. Is it true that you actually attacked your own son yesterday?"

"In a manner of speaking."

Jert McPhester shook his head. "And right after attacking Tump Walker on the handball courts. Duff, I'm sorry to say it, but I think you should seek professional help about your emotions. You're in serious trouble."

Duffy glanced at the office door, which Jert had left open. He put an expression on his face that he hoped looked contrite and troubled. "You mind if I close the door for a minute, Jert? I need to deal with something really serious."

Jert smiled fatly. "Anything to help you out, Duff."

Duffy closed the door, turned, and reached between Jert's legs, closing his nail-breaking hand around Jert's balls. He squeezed and pulled. Jert hunkered into a quarter squat and color leached from his face.

His voice, when it came, was a gasping whisper. "You goddam crazy sonofabitch." But he stood utterly still, because at his
slightest movement, Duffy brought more pressure to bear on
his balls.

"You even look like you're going to touch me," said Duffy,
"and I'm going to rip your nuts off. Understand?"

"Yes. Oh! Oh, yes!"

"Come with me," said Duffy. He led Jert around the desk.
Jert followed, stepping gingerly on tiptoe. Duffy took him around
three times before he stopped. "You do that very well," Duffy
said.

"Try to get control of yourself," whispered Jert, beginning
to slobber just a bit.

"*Get* control? Hell, I've *got* control, wouldn't you say, Jert?"
Enough pressure now to squeeze the juice out of a lemon.
"Wouldn't you?"

Jert danced a little jig. "Oh my God! Yes. You *are* in control.
All the way!"

"O.K. In that case, big fella, just step up here on this chair."
Duffy lifted and Jert followed as if by magic. When he was standing on the chair, Duffy said: "Now step over onto the desk." Jert
stepped and stood looking down at Duffy's hand where it held
him fast between the legs.

"For God's sake," whimpered Jert. "For God's sake."

"Now," said Duffy with some satisfaction, "what I want you
to do is crow like a rooster."

"Crow like a rooster?"

"Crow like a rooster."

"Cock-a-doodle-do," said Jert.

"I said *crow*," Duffy hissed, squeezing Jert's balls together
like two walnuts he meant to crack against each other.

"Oh, goddam!" cried Jert, going up on his tiptoes. Then he
threw back his head and crowed for all he was worth. "Cooooccckk-
aahhh-dooodddlle-doooooo."

"Better. Once more."

"Coooocccckk-aahhh-dooodddlle-doooooo."

58

Duffy watched the door. "Again," he said.

Jert crowed again, and Duffy turned him loose and stepped back from the desk as the secretary burst into the office, her thin mouth stretched, her eyes wide with fright. Jert stood on the desk, half hunkered now, his pale face gone slate gray.

"I heard . . ." said the secretary, "I thought I heard . . ." She did not seem able to say what she thought she heard.

Duffy looked at her and shook his head sadly. "He suddenly climbed up there and started crowing. I think he needs professional help." He winked. "Maybe you'd better call somebody. Know what I mean?"

"My God, yes," she said, rushing back toward her desk.

Jert, still hunkered around his wounded balls, was saying, "No. Mitzi, no. Don't call." But his voice was only a whisper and Duffy heard her talking frantically into the telephone as he sauntered out of the office and onto the stairs.

Duffy got into his Winnebago feeling considerably better. He took a bottle of Jack Daniel's from beside the seat, raised it to his mouth, and bubbled it twice to celebrate his victory. A minor one, to be sure, but a victory nonetheless. While he waited for the whiskey to take hold, he tried to think what to do next. Just about the time he became aware of the siren, he saw the Emergency Rescue paramedic ambulance, and two men sprinted into the building. Something made of heavy cloth with leather buckles all over it trailed from the hand of one of the men. Duffy bubbled the bottle again, and as he took it from his mouth he heard screaming from the law offices. Presently, Jert came springing out of the building, wearing a straitjacket. The two men from the ambulance were right behind him. One of them brought him down in a great open field tackle on the grass between the sidewalk and street. Jert was on his feet immediately. Even overweight and trussed up in a jacket, he still had the incredible balance that made him an All-American defensive end. As Jert was being hustled into the ambulance, he kept screaming: "Don't touch my balls! Watch the balls!"

So much for that. Let Jert McPhester explain standing on a

desk crowing like a rooster and his preoccupation with his balls. Duffy started the engine, and eased into the thin, midafternoon traffic. Without knowing where he was going, he drove directly to Marvella's apartment.

8

He let himself in with his own key, and from just inside the door he looked into the bedroom, where Marvella was naked in a four-point stance, with a young man riding her from behind. The boy stopped in midstroke to look at Duffy. Duffy again felt the wonderful lifting in his chest. At last something was working right. She thought he was off on vacation with Tish, so she had invited this boy whom Duffy had never seen before here for a nooner. What was more natural and right than that?

Duffy walked over to the bed and stuck out his hand. "My name's Duffy Deeter," he said.

The boy, on his knees, reached across Marvella's finely muscled back and shook his hand. "I'm Skipper. Skipper Frong."

"Frong," said Duffy. "Frong?"

"You probably know the name from seeing Frong's Chick'N'Fish. That's my daddy's chain."

Marvella had her neck twisted, looking over her shoulder watching them talk. Her eyes were tranquil, her face calm, as though she had been grazing there on her hands and knees.

"Tell your daddy he makes a hell of a sandwich," said Duffy.

"Duffy," she said, "do you mind? We're busy here."

"Thought you'd make a few puppies, did you?" said Duffy. "I'm going into the kitchen for something to eat." He slapped her lightly on the rump. "Take your time. I know where every-thing is."

Duffy made a turkey on rye with mustard and poured himself a glass of warm burgundy wine. Since he'd bubbled the bottle after going to the law offices, he'd been seriously considering getting drunk, bad drunk. Maybe he'd go out to a whiskey bar on the edge of town—and get the shit kicked out of himself. There was nothing so refreshing as getting your ass kicked. Duffy always felt purified and holy afterward. He chewed the sandwich slowly and listened to the pleasant, savage sound of slapping flesh in the next room.

While he was sipping his third glass of wine he heard the shower come on, and presently Skipper Frong and Marvella came into the kitchen, their hair damp, their faces flushed.

Skipper stuck out his hand. "Listen, I have to run now. Got to study for a humanities quiz. But it sure was nice meeting you."

Duffy shook his hand. "Good seeing you," said Duffy. "Maybe we'll cross again."

"Ditto," said Skipper Frong, and then he was gone.

Marvella sat down at the table and poured a glass of wine for herself. "You should have knocked."

"When did you ever know me to knock?"

"But, you know, when I think you're out of town, then you oughta knock. Jesus, that was awkward."

"I didn't mean to embarrass you."

"You didn't embarrass me. But one ought to observe a few decencies. Manners are all we have to protect us in this world."

"You take manners, I'll take a gun or a machete."

She reached across the table and pinched his cheek. "You violent, stone-crazy sweetheart. I love you."

"Of course you do."

"Would you like to tell me why you didn't go on vacation? What the fuck happened?"

He told her what happened, or at least he told her what

happened up to the time when his son was puking and Tish was screaming about seeing a lawyer.

"That's radical," she said. "Really rank."

"True. All the seams are unraveling in my life. But it's not as bad as it sounds."

"Bad enough. Sounds expensive too."

"You should know about expense, if anybody does. But I'm not beaten yet." He took a handful of Krugerrands out of his pocket and piled them on the table. "Those'll keep us going for a minute or two."

"Is that righteous gold?"

"Righteous it ain't, but gold it is."

She was suddenly agitated, squirming in her seat, pulling at her nose with thumb and forefinger. "Jesus, I'm gonna do up some coke. The sight of real money always makes my nose cold for coke."

There was a knock at the door.

"My God, Sweetcheeks, you've got'm lined up to get in here." He cupped his mouth and shouted toward the door. "Her box is booked up! Sold out! SRO!"

"Just when I think there's hope for you, you say something hopelessly middle-class." She had made no move to see who it was. "I don't know who the hell it is."

Whoever was there was really hammering now.

"You want to check it out, or do we just sit here and see how long we can stand it?"

She went to the door and unlocked it. There was a bellow of rage that Duffy recognized instantly as Jert McPhester's. Duffy turned to see him charging across the apartment toward him. His gait was strange, a little hunkered and skewed to the left.

Duffy deliberately relaxed in his chair and made himself look unconcerned, but he had his feet flat on the floor and he was prepared to move in any direction should it become necessary. Jert stopped at the end of the table. His mouth was working, but the sound he was making was all grunts and choking gags.

"You look like your shorts are too tight, Biggun," Duffy said.

"I'm taking you to court, you little bastard," Jert said, when he was finally able to speak. "I'd beat the life out of you if I didn't intend to sue you for assault."

"Just out of curiosity, how did you know where to find me?"

"You scum-sucking dog, you think everybody in town, including Tish, doesn't know you keep this whore up here?"

Marvella had picked up an apple and crushed a chunk out of it with her white perfect teeth. She chewed slowly and asked in a calm, disinterested voice: "You gonna let this fat dipshit call me a whore?"

Duffy gave her a smile of genuine affection. "Of course, darling. Nothing clears the air like the truth."

"You like the truth, do you?" gasped Jert. "Well, here's some more for you. I'll see you in court. I wanted to tell you to your face."

"Jert, are you really going to try to convince a judge and jury that your law partner took you by the balls and made you stand on a desk and crow like a rooster?"

Marvella put her apple down. "Say whuuut?"

"Tump Walker's suing you too. For a million dollars. He's got witnesses. I'm a fucking witness. How do you like that?"

Duffy said: "A million dollars? Does he want cash or will he take a check?"

"You've overloaded your ass this time, Duffy Deeter," said Jert. "There's no way out."

"Out?" said Duffy. "Out? Sweetheart, ain't none of us going out anywhere but six feet. And that's straight down."

Jert shook his head. "I still don't know why I don't kill you."

Duffy stood up. "Put your feet in the street. A psychotic urge is stealing in my brain, the urge to squeeze up on me a pair of balls."

There was an involuntary twitch in Jert's groin. He took a step backward, turned, and rushed out of the apartment, crying, "Madness! Madness!"

After Jert was gone, Marvella watched Duffy across the table. "Did you really take him by the balls and make him stand on a desk?"

"And crow like a rooster," said Duffy.

9

Marvella's nose vacuumed up another line. Duffy watched her, the ultimate consumer: cocaine, apples, sons of franchise owners, or whatever came to hand.

"Why you so quiet?" she said.

"I'm scheming," said Duffy.

"You want another line?"

"Cocaine bores the shit out of me. The only thing that bores me more than coke is people who do coke."

"*I'm* not boring," she said, her nose dripping snot clear as spring water.

"Have you talked to yourself lately?"

"You're not making any sense, Duffy." She sucked the snot off her upper lip and some more immediately reappeared. "You're not going to get freaky, are you? I think you're ready to slip straight into freaky."

"It's the season for freaky."

"Tell me again about the guy who's suing you for a million again."

He told her.

"No question," she said. "You slipped entirely into freaky."

"These are unusual times. They call for unusual measures. Are you with me?"

"That all depends," she said.

"Nothing depends, and that's the only thing we can depend on."

"What you got in mind?" she said.

"War," he said.

"War?"

"That's what it feels like."

"I'll need more coke for war." She giggled and bent to the mirror in front of her. When she raised back up again, she said, "These lines are the last I've got. Jesus, I'd like to get a half ounce to ward off the winter in case it comes."

"Have you got enough money to cover it? Until I get rid of the gold, I'm busted."

"Sure. It's only seven hundred for good shit that hasn't been walked to death."

Only seven hundred. God, she was expensive. But like the Winnebago, she was necessary. He was convinced that she was required for the sake of his sanity. And if that was what he thought, that was what was true. As Shakespeare said: Nothing is true or false but thinking makes it so.

"All right. I'll give you the money back. You go score what you need for the trip."

"What trip?"

"The one we're taking."

"Freaky and sweetly insane," she said. Duffy could see that her eyes were pinned and knew that she had severely warped herself with the coke. "Ding Dong Duffy, have you completely forgotten that I'm in school, for God's sake? When did you decide we were going on a trip?"

"Well, it's not something I just decided. I was going on a trip all along, remember? So I'm still going. It'll just be a little different trip from what I had thought at first, that's all."

"Where did you think to go?"

"I don't know."

"When you leaving?"

"I don't know. We'll leave when we leave."

"I'm not going."

"You'll do whatever I tell you to do."

"All right, Duffy."

That's the way it had been since he had met her and they had come to an understanding in Atlanta at a Bar Association meeting. She had recently been graduated from Auburn University in Alabama and was in the employ of a state senator who was also a lawyer. She was at the meeting to assist the senator and Duffy was at the meeting to distract himself from his marriage and his career and his life, all of which were going sour on him. She was young and beautiful and very frankly for sale. So he bought her and brought her to Gainesville. He only needed her when he needed her, and when he didn't she was free to do whatever she wished. Neither of them ever tried to pretend that what they had between them was anything but what it was. She generally struck him—whenever he thought about it at all— as being absolutely without substance. But, of course, the lack of substance was also some substance, wasn't it? As he looked at her now, the thought fluttered briefly in his skull again before he shook it loose.

"When you get back with the coke, get your shit together and be ready to go. I've got a few things to do myself."

"You mean selling the gold?"

"That and other things."

"What other things?"

"Places to go."

"Like where?"

"To search and destroy."

"I think I'll let that one alone," she said, licking the mirror clean. She stood up without another word and the door slammed behind her. Duffy knew that she was now on the scent of more cocaine, her nose was full of it, and she was incapable of thinking about anything else. The whole world could have been burning around her and she would not have noticed it.

Duffy took a shower and changed into fresh clothes from the stock he kept in her closet. He felt better now as he went down to his Winnebago and drove off through the late afternoon streets. Doing something, *anything*, always altered the day and put him in a better mood.

On University Avenue, seven blocks east of Main, he pulled into the parking lot of Poppandopolous's Gold Hole, a cinderblock building painted bright red, with foot-high white letters on all four sides that read: IF YOU WANT IT—WE'VE GOT IT! IF YOU'VE GOT IT—WE WANT IT! GOLD BOUGHT AND SOLD! BEST PRICES! The little building was like a fortress, its high, narrow windows barred with heavy steel. Duffy opened the door and saw Solomon Keppleman sitting where he always sat, at the back of the store at a plain, splintered desk in the dim light of a goosenecked lamp. He wore an eyeshade over round steel-rimmed glasses. Duffy walked down the aisle between long cases in which gold necklaces and coins and watches and pendants of every imaginable design gleamed behind a gridwork of steel secured by thick padlocks.

"Hello, Sol," said Duffy, stopping in front of the desk.

"Good day, Mr. Deeter," said Sol, turning his soft white hands palm up and giving a little shrug. It was a habitual gesture, one that went nicely with Mr. Keppleman's quiet, deferential voice.

Poppandopolous's Gold Hole had been here on University Avenue for as long as Duffy could remember and Solomon Keppleman had always owned it. "And what may Sol do for you, Mr. Deeter? Perhaps a little transaction?"

Duffy placed the velvet bag on the desk. The coins made the thick, satisfying *clink* of solid gold. Duffy had put them into the bag from this very desk six years before.

"Aaahhh," Sol breathed when he saw the color of gold. One of his hands did not so much touch as flutter over the neck of the bag. "How may I be of help?" His eyes had not moved from the bag.

"I need . . . " Duffy stopped. He had not thought about what kind of deal he wanted to do. "I need six thousand dollars." He could always come back if he needed to. "And I need it in cash. Now, this evening."

Duffy spilled some coins out onto the desk and put them in stacks of five. Duffy watched Solomon Keppleman watching the gold, his dry gray lips moving soundlessly now, tasting one another, as though he might be computing figures.

"Anything for you, Mr. Deeter," he murmured. "Anything at all. I could let you have six thousand dollars for twenty-two of your Krugerrands."

"Done," said Duffy.

Duffy put out four stacks of five and one stack of two and returned the rest of the coins to the bag. Solomon Keppleman came from around the desk. He was wearing bedroom slippers. He went to the front door and secured it with a double iron bar. When he came back he opened a Diebold safe and took a metal cashbox out onto his knees. Duffy was selling for less than three hundred dollars apiece and he'd bought at four-fifty. Still, he was not disappointed and he did not feel cheated. Just the opposite, really. He felt a solid rush of confidence and optimism as Solomon Keppleman counted bills onto the desk from the cashbox. Gold did not bullshit, and it never lied. Solomon had not asked why Duffy was selling at a loss, and Duffy had known that he wouldn't. And he had not inquired why Duffy wanted the money in cash instead of a check. Neither Solomon nor Duffy had to worry. Gold was good, a commodity that always gave the same answer.

Duffy counted the money and put it into his pocket.

"It's been a pleasure, Sol," he said.

"For you, anything anytime." He made the habitual gesture with his hands and shoulders. "Sol Keppleman is always glad to see you, Mr. Deeter."

He put the Krugerrands into the safe and then unbarred the front door for Duffy. The sun was down and it had cooled off some by the time he eased the Winnebago out of the parking lot and into traffic. He turned west on University Avenue and then north on Main for no particular reason. Marvella would not be back in the apartment yet and the notion of going back there to empty rooms did not appeal to him. He had no idea of what he wanted to do next until he passed an Eagle army-navy surplus store and he heard himself saying to Marvella: "To search and destroy."

He had not known at the time why he'd even said it, but now as he made a right U-turn back to the army-navy surplus store, he knew. Of course he wanted to search and destroy. He had been kicked out of his house, and his money had been taken from him. His life had been pillaged. He had said it was war and it was. The army-navy store seemed to be the place where he needed to be. He parked and went inside and, yes, this was the place, all right. He definitely needed jungle camouflage pants and shirt. And that black navy watch cap would fit his skull tightly. And shoes. Street shoes wouldn't do.

A young man with a noseful of broken veins had come to linger at his elbow. Duffy turned to him and said, "I need special shoes."

"Special shoes for what?"

"Creeping."

"Creeping?"

"And crawling."

"We have no creeping and crawling shoes, sir. If you wanted to jump out of an airplane, march in a rain forest, survive in the desert, or be warm in the Arctic, we could help you. Step back here and let me show you a little number for amphibious landings. I'm sure . . ."

He did not buy the shoes for amphibious landings, but he had wanted to. And he'd wanted the ones for the forest and jumping out of airplanes and surviving in the desert and hiking the frozen Arctic. The possibilities overwhelmed him. He dreamed over the shoes awhile, thinking of dripping forests and the cry of strange birds, listening to the howl of freezing wind and crunching snow.

Finally he decided that his Adidas would have to do. He did buy a web belt though, and a bayonet, a medicine kit, a canteen

71

and a Swiss survival knife. Might as well get *all* the stuff. Do it right. Go for it. Darkness had come while he was in the store, and he had to turn on the lights in the Winnebago to change into what he'd bought. The camouflage pants and shirt were stiff but they fit well. He checked himself in the mirror. Something was wrong. It was the face. He got out a can of black shoe polish and marked his cheekbones and chin, striped his forehead. That was better. The moon was out tonight and a white face would shine like a light in the dark.

He cut his motor half a block away and coasted into the trees at the top of the drive above the house. The lights from the living room showed him Tish's car in the garage, and there beside it was Jert's red Corvette. The sound of the blaring TV drifted up to him. He checked his watch. Two minutes to nine. He took off the watch and left it on the dashboard in front of the steering wheel.

He stepped out of the Winnebago and into the trees, and moved over the moon-dappled leaves like a shadow. At a window where the curtains did not quite meet he pressed his face to the glass. Through the triangle of light, he could see through the kitchen and dining room and into the living room. The dispirited lump of his son sagged in front of the television set. He was eating something out of a box, his chubby jaws working in a slow, steady rhythm.

But where were Tish and Jert? The lights in the other end of the house were on and he turned to watch them. As if on a signal, the one in the master bedroom went out. He walked quietly down to the end of the house. Sliding glass doors opened directly onto the terrace from all the bedrooms. He lightly vaulted the wooden railing and stopped by the glass door behind which he had spent so many miserable nights. He heard the sloshing and lapping of his huge water bed and a low murmuring of voices, a murmuring that turned to grunts and snorts even as he listened. And then the sound of slobbering that could only be Jert. Ah, Jesus, the kid was out there in front of the

TV getting sadder and fatter, blowing up on commercials, and back here in the dark, Tish and Jert might be making another one in a single sweaty nocturnal spasm. But not likely. Tish would have her plug in. Or maybe she wouldn't. Maybe they wanted a bunch of little Jerts. How utterly goddam depressing. They needed help. And he, Duffy Deeter, would help them. He'd come to creep, creep and lurk, and by God he would. He moved down to the glass door that went into his son's room. He took the Swiss survival knife out of his pocket and forced the lock. He moved out into the hall and down to the room he used as a study. He wasn't worried about noise. The roaring sound of the TV reverberated through the house. His son's hearing was probably permanently damaged anyway from long stunned hours of listening to crashing cars, gun battles, and screaming singers. In the study, he went straight to his old fraternity paddle, which hung from the wall on a leather strap. He looped the strap around his wrist, hefted the paddle, and took a few smooth swings. It was a monster of a board. Three feet long, seven inches wide, with four holes bored through the end of it. Duffy had raised blisters the size of strawberries with it on the asses of pledges.

He went down the hall to the bedroom. He touched the doorknob. It was not locked. Strange. Tish had always locked the door during his own ruttings. Locked it against poor Felix. He'd never thought to wonder why, since Felix was generally immobile anyway. He eased the door open. In the darkened room, the huge thrusting rump of Jert seemed to set even the walls in violent motion.

"Gunch," growled Jert. "Gunch! Gunch!" His grinding teeth made him sound as if he might be eating glass.

Tish groaned. "Drive, you big sonofabitch, drive!"

It had been a very long time since Duffy had heard her sound like that and it made him remember lying in the grass with her that night by the wall of the Castillo de San Marcos. He felt his heart turn with a strange coldness. But only for a moment. For a long time now he had known that Tish had a thousand voices, all of them practiced, all of them phony.

He could see nothing of her but two smooth rounded knees vibrating like tuning forks. Old Jert really had her pinned to the mat. Duffy positioned himself at the foot of the water bed and contemplated the enormous globes of Jert's ass. He looked down at the vague outlines of the long paddle he was holding. He drew back, took careful aim and swung, shifting his hips to get the full force of his body behind the blow.

The sweet, satisfying *splat* of wood on flesh bounced off the oak-paneled walls. Jert stiffened and screamed, thrashing at the bedclothes like a drowning swimmer. But before he could move, Duffy caught him in the ass with another shot, which caused Jert to lunge forward and ram his head into the wall in front of him.

Tish was screaming, "What in the world? What in the world?" And Jert was howling like a dog as Duffy slipped out of the room and back down the dark hall, at the end of which he could see the inconstant light of the flickering television and hear Felix cheering over the sound of crashing cars and gunfire.

On the way back up the hill to the Winnebago, Duffy thought about what he had done and it came to him as a headline in tomorrow's newspaper: LOCAL MAN HITS WIFE'S LOVER IN ASS WITH BOARD. How would that look? Well, goddammit, it would look wonderful, wouldn't it? Men everywhere would applaud.

In the Winnebago, he scrubbed the shoe polish off his face, took off his web belt, and changed out of his camouflaged clothes. While he was changing, the thought occurred to him that what he had just done might be of more significance than just the satisfaction it had brought. It might be some sort of turning point in his life. It sort of felt that way. But even as he thought it, doubt came sliding right in behind it. He wasn't sure. (Would anything ever be sure again?) He needed confirmation, needed to talk it over. And there was joy in his heart that he knew exactly where to go to talk about such a thing.

Thank God for mothers. Or at least for *his* mother. Hers was an understanding that passeth understanding. He liked that, and as he roared along the streets and whipped around the corners, he sang it out, over and over again: "Understanding that passeth understanding."

10

"Dip the goldfish, son."

"I'm dipping them, Mom."

"Well," said the old lady, "dip'm."

"A little more light would help," he said.

"What? How's that?"

"Light," he said, raising his voice. "I could do this better if I had a little more light."

"Have you dropped any?"

"I don't think so."

"Don't drop my goddam goldfish."

With a tiny net no bigger than a teacup, Duffy dipped tiny goldfish out of bowls and placed them in a wide shallow dishpan. His mother sat across the room by the window, which was covered with heavy brown curtains. All the windows in the apartment were covered with the same kind of curtains. They had hung over the windows in the house she had lived in before Duffy had moved her here to a condominium on the seventh floor of the tallest building in Gainesville. She had seemed lonely in the house after his father died, and it had always been dark and stuffy. He had moved her here to Golden House, where a hundred other old people lived, so that she could have lots of air and light and friends and not be lonely.

But it had not worked out. She kept the place sealed and dark, and her only friends were goldfish. Hundreds of tiny goldfish in glass bowls scattered about the apartment.

"You ought to take better care of these things, Mom," he said, searching for a fish in a cloudy bowl.

"I take precious care of the goddam fish," his mother said. She had taken up cursing with a vengeance when she found her husband dead.

Duffy thrashed through the milky water with his little net. "This water needs changing," he said.

Duffy heard her snort all the way across the room from where she sat, a tiny bundle of closely wrapped housecoats, a dim outline in front of the heavy curtain covering a window that gave onto an endless view of Payne's Prairie. That view had cost Duffy a lot of dollars. He wondered if she had ever seen it.

She snorted again and said, "I fucking despair of you ever knowing anything."

Duffy found the little fish he had been searching for in the bowl. It was dead. He put the fish in his pocket. It was the tenth one he'd found. He could feel the weight of them in his pocket, damp against his leg.

"What are you doing?" she demanded.

"What?" he said. He thought she'd seen him putting the goldfish in his pocket.

"Are you dipping them out to change the water or what? If you're not, what in the hell are you doing? And if you are, why are you telling me the water needed changing? Honestly, Duffy, you sometimes remind me of your father before he bit the big bagel."

Bit the big bagel was an expression of hers. She had many such expressions. They had come on her, along with cursing, when she found her husband dead. Duffy dipped up a semicomatose fish and dropped it in the dishpan, where it didn't turn belly up but kind of lay on its side.

"You don't seem like yourself today," his mother said. "Are you yourself today?"

He could feel her staring at him and he stopped with the fish to consider the question. It struck him as a perfectly good question.

"I'm O.K.," he said finally, which was not the same thing as answering the question. He felt his confidence eroding. He was beginning to feel mushy at his center.

"I know what you've got," the old lady snorted. It seemed she couldn't talk without snorting. He couldn't remember her ever doing it when he was a child.

He looked at her, half afraid that she did, in fact, know what he had, and worse, that she was about to name it.

"Problems," she barked, "that's what you got. Now come over here and sit down."

He put the little net beside the dishpan full of sick and dying goldfish and went to sit on a chair in front of his mother.

"Now," she said, "it all started when your father named you Duffy. You were still in the hangar, if you get my drift, and he says to me, he says, 'We'll name it Duffy.'"

Her eyes were bright and the skin of her face was tight and smooth as bone.

"I'm having a little trouble at home," Duffy said, and felt the old surge of confidence.

"So I said to your father, I said, 'What kind of name is Duffy?'"

"I made my son puke," Duffy said.

"I told him that Duffy was no fit name for a daughter."

Duffy said, "And Tish seems to be fucking Jert." He was really beginning to feel good now that he was talking about it, getting it all out in the open.

"And your father said, 'It won't be a daughter and we'll name it Duffy.'"

"No," said Duffy, "Tish *is* fucking Jert. That is one thing I'm sure of."

Saying a thing he was sure of helped. It sent an unnameable happiness pinging along in his blood.

"Your father was not wrapped real tight," she said. "His loaf was missing several slices."

"And I *did* hit Jert in the ass with a board," said Duffy. "Nobody can argue with that. It is a fact."

"Your father was a fine man," she said, showing him her teeth. One of her canines was filigreed with gold. She thought the gold made her false teeth look more like the real thing, which it did. "A fine man, all right. It's too bad he was three bricks shy of a load."

He smiled and took her hand. "Well, at least you and I are sound, Mom. Solid as a rock."

She frowned and jerked her head. The sudden movement made her teeth click. "I didn't say he wasn't sound. And I didn't say he wasn't solid." She took her hand away from his. "They just put him in a plane and he killed five men and never got over it. Because war is legal. That's what done him in, it being legal. If he'd caught'm in an alley and cut their throats and they'd put him in jail for life, he'd a been fine. But he shot'm out of the sky and instead of putting him in jail, they gave him a medal. That's what he couldn't stand, the sonofabitch. It made him look funny out of his eyes for the rest of his life."

Oh, Jesus, thought Duffy, we're back to that. Back to the planes.

Duffy stood up. "I've got to finish with the goldfish."

His mother got out of her chair with surprising speed and agility for a woman of seventy-three. "We're talking planes, goddammit. Talking your sweet bastard father before he lost it, dropped the goddam load. Bring your young ass on back here. It won't hurt you to remember your father."

"I don't need to see it," Duffy said. "I haven't forgotten him."

But he followed her anyway as she led him to the back of the apartment. She stood in front of a door and took a single breath before opening it. And there it was. His father's room, or, as he had called it, his hangar. She'd had everything transported from the room he died in at the old house and put back together here in Golden House condominium. The same heavy curtains that covered the other windows covered these, and all through the dim light flew planes in every angle of attack, diving, banking, climbing and spiraling in the thick, dead air of the sealed room.

She touched a switch on the wall and the light caught the thin wires from which the planes were suspended from the ceiling. American fighters, P-51 Mustangs and P-47 Thunderbolts and P-40 Warhawks swarmed in a static dogfight with German BF109 Messerschmitts and FW190 Focke-Wulfs. Bombers— Flying Fortresses and Liberators and Marauders and Black Widows—flew in tight formations while escort fighters, waspish and deadly, swarmed about them.

Duffy looked at them as he always had, with awe and a kind of horror, but with envy too, for the men who had flown the planes in combat. What a wondrously murderous thing to have done. Talk about a goddam answer that did not admit of bullshit. One on one at ten thousand feet with twenty-millimeter cannon would surely leave a man purified and holy. What a feeling that must have been, and his father, blood of his blood, had known it. But it had been too much for him, and he had spent the years after World War II in a room much like this one, building these planes, exact replicas in precise scale, hanging them and watching them fly, gazing endlessly at his dreams and terrors.

Duffy's mother had been standing utterly still, staring at the planes the way a snake might stare at a bird. She had handled all those years wonderfully, collecting her husband's disability pension out of the mailbox every month and running the house and her life with great efficiency, never objecting to the old man's obsession, or even to the sounds of engines that often roared out of his mouth or the bomb bursts or crackling gunfire that exploded around his tongue sometimes in the early hours of night.

Until she found him dead. She had found him collapsed face down at his worktable, his face buried in the half-finished skeleton of the plane he was building when his heart stopped. It was a P-38 Lightning fighter. The plane he had flown in the war. The one he went down in over France. The one that brought the disability pension every month, and brought also the obsession every waking and dreaming minute of his life.

There was his worktable against the far wall, and on it was the crushed P-38 she'd found his face in.

She turned her eyes, bright as wet glass, on Duffy. "Well, goddammit, don't just stand there. What do you think?"

"I think you ought to get rid of this shit," he said bitterly, and the bitterness surprised him. He thought he'd long since got past this. The tried to think of Tao. Concentrate his heart in Zen. Couldn't. In the moment it was gone.

"Oh, no," she said lightly. "I want to see his face there in that mashed plane where I found it."

"That's cruel," Duffy said.

"No, that's . . ." Her voice broke off and she turned with a suddenness that startled Duffy and threw her arms around him and hugged him to her with a strength that he could never have imagined she had. "Whhhyyyy?" she screamed, a single, long wailing cry that might have been that of a child. "Oh, why! Where is what we had? Where is the sonofabitch? I love him. I hate him. I love to hate him and, damn the poor sweet bastard, how I hate to love him. Whhyy? Can't you tell me why?"

Not only could Duffy not answer why, he could not even speak. His heart and mind were empty of words.

And just as suddenly as she screamed, she stopped. When she drew away from him, her face was composed, her eyes dry.

"What in the hell have you got in your pocket?" she demanded. She looked down. "It's wet."

Duffy said, "I don't . . ."

"Don't lie to me, young man. Let me see."

Because he did not know what else to do, Duffy slowly drew a handful of goldfish out of his pocket.

"My God, I've raised an idiot," she said. "You don't put goldfish in your pocket when you change the water."

"They're dead," said Duffy.

"Change the water and put'm back in anyway. How do you know dead goldfish don't like clean water?"

Duffy could only look at her. He had no answer.

"Then that's a lock, right?" she said.

"That's a lock, Mom."

That's a lock. Prison slang, for Christ's sake, or at least it had been before it got into the street. And hadn't she heard anything he'd said about Tish and Felix and Jert? In his heart he felt certain she had. Heard and understood. But maybe at her age and in her world, things like making your son puke, and slapping your wife's lover in the ass with a board while they were fucking were all just incidental, beside the point. He didn't think for a minute that she was crazy, although he knew there were other people who did. Duffy wondered if she had only seen through to the other side of a place he himself had never been privileged to see.

He followed his mother out of the room and took his little net and went back to work on the bowls of dead and dying goldfish.

11 When Duffy left his mother's apartment at Golden House, a misting rain was falling, and it had cooled off. West of Gainesville, off toward the Gulf of Mexico, heat lightning flashed low on the horizon. As Duffy eased through the fog rising out of the steaming streets, his ears were full of the sound of his father's voice and his eyes swarmed with banking, diving fighter planes. He had not wanted to go into his father's room, his hangar, but he had and now the planes would not leave him alone, nor would the memory of his father. Duffy did not want to think about the old man's world because there was no help for any of that, no help for what happened to his father and what he became because of it. But what he wanted to do was beside the point. Duffy *would* think of him, just as he knew he would drive east on Eighth Avenue to Waldo Road and then north to the airport.

He stopped at a package store and bought a bottle of Wild Turkey, not because he much wanted it but because it was his father's favorite whiskey. In the parking lot, with the mist still falling, he uncapped the bottle, raised it in a toast and said: "Here's to you, old man." He pulled long and hard at the whiskey before lowering the bottle.

"Duffy," he said to himself, "you are a sentimental asshole, and he would not approve. No, *he* would not approve."

He drove out of the parking lot onto Waldo Road and tried to tell himself it was the whiskey causing the tears that blurred his vision. Aw, what the fuck. So he missed his father, so what? He loved the old man, had always loved him, even when he was ashamed of him. In the distance, Duffy saw the blinking lights of a descending plane and heard the roar of the engines, and even though he tried not to, he saw his father's hands dogfighting one another.

For Duffy, the old man had been a wonderful father because Duffy was an only child and his father had been a perfect playmate. All the rooms and halls of the huge house had echoed with laughter and the sound of planes and gunfire and exploding bombs. It was a two-story gabled Victorian house Duffy's mother had bought with money her family had settled on her at the time of her marriage, the same money that would later send Duffy through law school. The ceilings of the rooms were high, and in Duffy's memory a bright flood of light forever poured through the wide windows. It was only after his father's death that the light was shut out with heavy curtains.

Duffy parked the camper on the shoulder of the road and watched a plane, running lights blinking, make its landing approach. He opened the bottle of Wild Turkey and took another drink as the plane passed low over him with the deep rushing sound of dragging flaps.

"Flaps down," his father would say.

"Flaps down, Dad," Duffy confirmed, pushing the handle of a toy hammer forward in his lap.

The two of them were sitting on the floor in the hallway in a bright square of moonlight falling through the window behind them. Duffy had awakened a half hour earlier, with his father kneeling by his bed.

"Time to fly," his father had said.

"Yes, sir," said Duffy, swinging his feet to the floor. He was barefoot and wearing the red gown with little pearl buttons his mother had made for him, and he followed his father out to the flight line to inspect the plane they were about to fly on a mission. After they had walked around the imaginary plane tied down in the living room, they talked to the imaginary pilots about the flight plan and the weather they could expect and the enemy that would come to meet them as the bombers they were escorting approached their target. None of what they heard from the other pilots was ever good. Invariably, the flight plan had been made by the wing commander, who was a fool, the weather was bad, and they were outnumbered by aircraft with superior firepower. But they flew anyway. They always flew, no matter what.

With the flaps down, they were making their approach and his father was talking frantically to the tower because they were badly shot up. The stabilizer was damaged, no longer functioning, the left wing tip was shot off, and the hydraulic system was out so that they had no landing gear.

"Tower, this is niner seven niner," his father said, his voice tense, "final approach."

"Niner seven niner," his father said, his voice now the calm, assured voice of the tower speaking back to himself, "crash crew is out, foam is down, come on home."

"Hold her steady," he cried to Duffy. "This is it."

Duffy held her steady with the handle of the little hammer in his lap. His father threw back his head and out of his mouth came the high, whining sound of their crippled, descending plane. The two of them bumped and slammed about there in the square of moonlight on the floor of the hallway with his father making the metal-scraping racket of a belly landing. His father's face was shining with sweat now, but when he spoke his voice was steady.

"We kicked ass and took names, Duffy."

"Dad, we something, all right, you and me."

Out of the dim light at the end of the hall, as silent as a ghost, Duffy's mother appeared. Her long white gown had a blue bow at the neck and about her mouth played the beginnings of a smile. She made a little clucking sound as she came toward them.

"Get out of the cockpit, Henry," she said.

"We were lucky to get back," he said.

She took his hand and helped him to his feet. "Are you all right?"

"If I'm talking, I'm alive, and if I'm alive, I'm O.K."

"We're good as can be, Mom," Duffy said, "but we lost the wheels on this one."

"Come on," she said. "Let's go down to the kitchen and I'll make both of you some hot chocolate."

When she turned on the light in the kitchen, his father stopped and slowly looked around him, examining the stove carefully and then the refrigerator.

"I see they've got a coffeemaker just like ours," he said.

His mother was spooning cocoa into a pot and did not look up. "Yes, they do, Henry, just like ours."

"How long did they say we could live here?" he asked.

She quit with the cocoa and took his shoulders in her hands. "Henry, I've talked to them, and they said we could live here as long as we like. They said we were to use the house just like it was ours."

"Well, thank God for that," he said.

Duffy took another hit of the Wild Turkey and watched a plane taxi toward the terminal. Those years before he had started to school were wonderful but things had gone bad the first day on the playground with the other children. At first, Duffy did not even know what his playmates were saying. Then he realized they were talking about his father, and more than that, they were saying dreadful things. They were saying his father was crazy, calling him the Red Baron and the Mad Bomber. And because of what they were saying, Duffy had his first fight on the first day he started school. Duffy had hit a kid twice and there was blood trickling from his nose before Duffy realized what he had done. And the word went out from there that Duffy Deeter would go stone crazy and bite, gouge and kick anybody who said anything about his father's obsession with airplanes. Consequently, the other children had learned never to say anything about his father where Duffy could hear it, but he always knew, or thought he knew, they were talking behind his back, and he had come to be ashamed of the father he loved.

Duffy cranked up the Winnebago and drove down Waldo Road to the entrance to the airport. He stopped by the terminal and sat watching as an Eastern Airlines jet touched down. He picked up the bottle from the seat beside him and then put it down again. The whiskey was not working. It fell on his stomach like water. The rain had stopped. He got out of the camper and went to stand by the fence.

He had stood at this very fence with his father three weeks before he had the massive coronary that killed him. They were watching the Greater Gainesville Air Show. It was November, on a Saturday. The chill air shook with the roar of revving engines, and above them against a cloudless sky a biplane was doing an inside loop, trailing smoke. His mother was not with them. She hated airplanes and could not bear the notion of seeing the aircraft that had been advertised for the show: gull-winged Corsairs and B-29 Superfortresses and Japanese Zeros, all manner of planes, including the P-38 his father had been shot down in.

"I don't want to go," his mother had said at breakfast, repeating what she'd been saying for a week. "And I'd rather you didn't go either."

"You know how long it's been since I saw a P-38?" his father said.

Duffy was concentrating on buttering his English muffin, but he still saw his mother flinch when his father said the name of the plane.

"I know how long it's been, Henry," she said.

"It's such a beautiful day and I just thought it would be a lot of fun for Duffy and me to be out there together," his father said. "An outing for all of us if you'll come."

"I won't come, Henry," she said. "I don't like that . . . that . . . all that *noise*."

Duffy, only twelve at the time, wanted to go, wanted it badly, because he wanted to see a real P-38. So far, he only knew them from the models he had been building with his father for years.

"We won't stay very long, Mom," Duffy said. And then: "We'll be fine. We won't have any trouble at all."

Duffy knew what was really on his mother's mind, what she was worried about. His father had been quiet at night lately, and even during the day he had been on his best behavior. But could she trust him to go to the air show without her, and to take Duffy with him as well? Duffy knew she wanted to believe that she could, because she wanted desperately to believe that her husband was getting better. For as long as Duffy could remember, she had been hinting, sometimes saying outright, that she thought her husband was getting stronger. *Stronger,* that was her word, but what she meant was that he would—one day soon—quit spending his days in the hangar. Quit bombing and strafing the house at night.

"Go then," his mother said. "Just the two of you. I have more than enough to keep me busy here today."

And, God, it had been a great day. Hot dogs and coke. Veterans of Foreign Wars in their blue-and-gold caps talking in front of the aircraft, their hands going ninety miles to the minute, banking, rolling, stalling, looping and diving. Martial music with lots of tubas and drums coming from the loudspeakers. Duffy had wandered through it all with his father, whose eyes were bright with an excitement that Duffy had never seen in them before.

And his father had talked nonstop of planes: of the P-51 Mustang that came into the war in 1944 and was the only fighter that could escort bombers out of England all the way to Berlin; of the B-29 that dropped the atom bomb; of the German Heinkel HE111 that fought in the Battle of Britain against British Spitfires and Hurricanes; and of the F4U Corsair that carried four twenty-millimeter cannons and had underwing racks for eight rockets.

Duffy was dizzy with the names of planes and their armament when they finally came to stand in front of his father's old plane, the P-38. Abruptly, his father fell silent. His bright eyes went brighter. His face flushed. Duffy waited for him to say something. But he did not.

"Did you like it, Dad?" Duffy said. It was something Duffy had long suspected.

His father looked as if he had been offered a snake to hold. "What?"

"You liked it, didn't you? You liked it all."

He said: "It was the most terrible thing in the world. It was the most wonderful thing in the world."

"And you liked it," Duffy said, making it a statement.

"Yes, I liked it."

"You think I'd like it, Dad?" And then, when he didn't answer: "Do you?"

He turned and walked away from the P-38. He never looked back when he spoke. "You'll find out soon enough, son. Every man's time comes to him, and yours will come to you. It doesn't really matter if you go to war or not. In the nation of the heart, there's enough war for everybody."

Duffy pushed himself away from the fence and spat into the damp grass. There was a sour taste at the root of his tongue. It had started misting again. He went back to the Winnebago and uncapped the Wild Turkey. He took a drink against the sour taste in his mouth and then sat behind the wheel staring at the label. He could hear his father's voice as plainly as he had heard it that day at the air show: "You'll find out soon enough, son. Every man's time comes to him, and yours will come to you."

But his time had not come to him. Despite the fact that he could run all day and was hard as a rock, something as absurd as a history of asthma had kept him out of Vietnam. Instead of going to war, he had gone to college on his mother's money.

But his father had been right, he thought bitterly: not going to war was also going to war.

He tried not to think of the planes and of the men doing battle, one with the other. But he thought of them anyway. That was the price for going into his father's old room. As he had known it would be when his mother insisted he visit it with her.

12   Duffy parked the camper and sprinted up the steps to Marvella's apartment. There was a light under the door, but that didn't necessarily mean she was home. When Marvella got into a long-range supply of cocaine, all guarantees went out the window.

He let himself in with his key, and through the lighted doorway of the bedroom he saw Tump Walker, as blackly shiny as a wet seal, sitting on the floor propped up on one elbow, a mirror beside him covered with lines of coke. Tump held a rolled-up bill between his thumb and forefinger. Marvella sat cross-legged on the bed above him and even from where Duffy stood he could see that her eyes were pinned from the dope, her beautiful mouth a little slack and silly.

Tump glanced briefly at Duffy and then bent and vacuumed up a line through the bill.

"I was beginning to think you weren't coming home, little brother," Tump said, rising to his feet in a single fluid motion that was like magic.

"My fucking name's Duffy, not little brother." The sight of Tump, which made absolutely no sense at all, cleared Duffy's head. Whatever it was, it was a new challenge. And he told himself he was ready for it.

Tump said, "I know your name, man."

"Good," said Duffy. "At least we got that straight."

Duffy looked from Tump to Marvella and back again, so many questions ticking through his mind that he didn't know where to start. Tump was immaculate in white shorts, socks and shoes, and wearing a light blue knit shirt of some very thin material that looked as if it was painted on him. The shirt was cut in a deep V halfway to his navel, and Duffy thought he had enough gold chains hanging around his neck to pull a truck loaded with hogs out of a ditch.

Marvella swung her long fine legs off the side of the bed and said: "Tish called."

"Tish called here?"

"Twice," said Marvella. "She was hysterical."

Tump picked up the mirror, put it on a little table, and sat in a chair beside it.

"How the hell do you know she was hysterical?"

Marvella walked over and took the rolled bill out of Tump's hand and did a line. "Because that's what she said. I'm hysterical. She said it both times she called. She said for you to call her back just as soon as you came in."

Tump waved one of his finely muscled hands toward Duffy. "It looks like you in deep enough here without me, man . . . Duffy. I ain't here with grief. I was just over town scoring a little crank for myself and Marvella. . . . Hey, ain't this girl got a name? One of the sisters' names. Anyhow, she walks in and I don't know her from jump street but she hears one of the brothers call my name and she knows me and we got to talking—"

"Hysterical and she wants *me* to call her?" said Duffy.

"—and I just wanted to come over and tell you I'm sorry about the tooth, man. Jesus, a fucking tooth. Lost a couple myself and it's something about losing a tooth, you know what I'm saying? So fucking permanent-like. Ribs, a shoulder, even a mothering knee can heal. But teeth don't heal."

Tump was on a coke babble and Duffy knew it. But there

was something about the guy coming over to the apartment and apologizing for the tooth that he liked very much.

"The tooth shit doesn't bother me," said Duffy. "I'll get by it." He wondered if he ought to do a line to cut back against the alcohol before he called Tish. "That heel that caught you in the head wasn't an accident. I meant to do it."

"Hey, I ain't a fool, white boy. I know that. See, I was just goofing, bored. It was supposed to be a joke or something. I don't know. Just goofing."

"I guess Marvella told you I know about the million-dollar lawsuit."

"She told me Jert said that to you."

"That's what he said."

Tump showed him some white, even teeth, incredibly white, except for two of them on the left side of his mouth. They were gold. "And you believed him." It was a statement, not a question. "He told you that, and you believed him."

Duffy said, "I believe everything. I'm the world's champion believer."

"Duff, come over here and do up some dust," Tump said. "Your whole brain's twisted."

"You sure as hell called my brain right, and I don't know if I need anything up my nose, but I'll blow some anyway. It looks to be a long night."

"Man, if I sued every guy who ever turned my lights out, I wouldn't have time to do anything else. Wonder what made Jert say a thing like that."

Duffy considered telling Tump about squeezing Jert's balls, then thought better of it. "He's big on personal injury, Jert is."

Tump gave him the teeth again. "Shit, man, *I'm* big on personal injury. Any hardass in the NFL can tell you that."

"That's not exactly what I meant. I meant . . ."

"I know what you meant, Duff. It was a fucking joke. I didn't just go to practice in college, I went to class too. The black dog's got you chewed to the bone. Looked at you when you came in, knew you was knee deep in heavyweight blues."

93

"Where the hell were you so long?" said Marvella.

"I went by to see Mom."

Tump wagged his huge, finely chiseled head. "I like a man that goes to see his mama. I *do* like that. You goin' to do up some of this shit or not? Why don't you do up and lighten up?"

The phone rang and Duffy snatched the rolled bill out of Tump's fingers and blew two quick lines.

Marvella didn't move from where she sat on the bed. "You might as well get it, Duffy. It's her again."

Duffy picked up the phone.

"Hello."

"Duffy, you've got to come over here right away." It was Tish, but she seemed calm enough to him.

"Sorry, Tish. But Jert said you had a court order that . . ."

"For Christ's sake, Duffy. Forget that shit. We've been robbed, and—"

"Robbed. You and Felix were robbed?"

Hesitation, and then: "Jert was here. Somebody came in and . . . It was just terrible."

"I'm not the police," said Duffy. "Call the fucking police."

"I've already done that. Duffy, please. Felix is here. That person may come back."

"I don't even know why you're calling me. And I don't see what I could do anyway."

"You could come. And you're my husband, that's why I'm calling you."

By God, she did sound a little hysterical, her voice getting tight and shrill there toward the end.

"Take some of the money you got out of the bank and hire yourself a security guard."

"Duffy, I was angry when I did that. I was just trying to get back at you." Her voice had gone lower, pleading. "If you can't think about me, think about Felix."

"Nobody in his right mind would kidnap Felix," said Duffy. "Who'd ransom a kid like that?" He didn't mean that, and he knew it. He'd give his life for poor fat Felix.

"Duffy, you're a cruel sonofabitch."

"Sometimes. But cruelty is kindness. You ought to know that. You really ought to know that."

"My God, you really do believe that shit you're always talking."

The thought came to him with sudden awful clarity that, no, he did not believe it. But then somewhere inside his head he heard a voice, his own voice, speaking flatly and trancelike, saying: "No belief is also some belief. Nonbelief *is* belief."

"Forget about what I said. Is Jert still there?"

"He's talking to the police."

"I'll come over," he said. This was, in its way, wonderful. He wished he could take his mother with him. This was the kind of twisted shit that she saw right to the heart of.

"Are you coming right away?"

"Right away." He hung up the phone.

"Is Jert *where?*" said Tump, bending to a line of coke.

"My wife's house."

"Was he?" Marvella asked. "What the hell's going on?"

"I've got to go over there. She says somebody broke in and attacked them. Jert's there. The cops are there. God knows who else. And she insists on me coming over. Something about the kid."

"I thought she was divorcing you," Marvella said. "I thought she had a restraining order on—"

Duffy said, "Marvella, you coked-out cunt—"

"Damn, you talk ugly," said Tump.

"—try to concentrate, look at my face. Do I look like I know what the fuck's going on?"

"I didn't mean anything," she said.

"I know that," said Duffy. "You don't mean *anything*."

"That's cold," said Tump. "That's really cold, Duffy."

Duffy held his hands out, palms down. "So sit tight. I'll be back before you know I'm gone. Then we'll take it from there."

He headed for the door and had his hand on the knob before

he realized that Tump was right behind him, so smoothly did the big man move across the floor.

"You leaving?" asked Duffy.

"I'm going with you."

"You're nuts, man. This could be bad stuff. And it doesn't concern you."

"Jert concerns me. Talking shit in the street with my name on it. *He* concerns me. He's there, so I'm going with you."

Tump's great dark eyes were turning sixes and sevens and the coke was making him grind his teeth. A forked vein stood out on his forehead above the bridge of his nose. The dope had him breathing as if he'd been doing wind sprints.

"You can see him tomorrow."

"I may be dead tomorrow. I want to see him now. Nothing heavy. I promise. You got my word, nothing heavy. I only want to tell the man that Tump Walker speaks for himself." He smiled. "Besides, I'm beginning to feel like I owe you a little something for yesterday. For the tooth. If it comes down just right, you may need a backup."

"I don't know, Tump."

"*I* know. And I'm the only one that has to know. O.K.?"

That settled it for Duffy. He liked that kind of talk. He needed to hear some of it, needed to be warmed a little from the kind of heat that only comes from confidence.

"O.K.," said Duffy. "But for God's sake, try to calm down. There's cops over there." He was worried about Tump, about how close to the edge he seemed to be. "Cops. Remember cops? The guys with the badges and guns."

"I'll cool out on the ride over."

"It's not a long ride," Duffy said.

"I'm a fast cool." Tump showed him his two gold teeth.

Duffy opened the door.

"All right if I do a few more of these lines of yours, Tump, while you gone?"

"Do all you want, sister," Tump said over his shoulder. "But take it from a pro. Your stem's twisted tight enough already."

96

13

On the ride over, Duffy started to tell Tump about the whole thing, squeezing balls and all. But he didn't. The thing that stopped him was that he didn't know how to begin. Hitting a guy in the ass while he was fucking? Was that crazy? That was probably crazy. Duffy didn't mind being thought crazy. But he did mind being thought a fool. Maybe only a fool would have done what he did.

"None of my business, Duff, but what's Jert doing at your old lady's house this time of night?"

"You're right. It's none of your business. But I could give a shit. He's going to represent her when she files for divorce against me."

"My, my," said Tump. "You like a box of Cracker Jacks. Every time your lid gets lifted, another surprise jumps out. I thought he said he was your law partner."

"He is. Was."

"That's warped."

"Now you got everything right."

They rode a few blocks in silence.

"You ought to see about getting that tooth fixed," said Tump.

"That's what my wife said."

"She's right. Man ought to keep his mouth pretty, and put

together. A fucking broken tooth," Tump said, shaking his head. "I hate a broken tooth. Teeth don't heal."

"So you told me."

They drove on in silence, and when they turned into the drive two police cars were parked there, blue top lights spinning and flashing.

"Good-looking house you got here, man," said Tump.

"Had, Tump, had. It's Tish's now."

"You giving it to the bitch?"

"The courts will if she goes through with the divorce. Don't ever get divorced in Florida. Shittiest state in the Union for a divorce if you're a fucking man. Remember that, Tump, when the time comes."

Tump had the door open and was getting out when he stopped briefly and looked back over his shoulder. "Time comes? You got to get married to need a divorce. This is one mother's son who won't ever be caught carrying a sandwich to a banquet."

"Tump, why couldn't I've met you ten years ago? You could have saved me a lot of grief."

"Well, you met me now. And I *still* might be able to save you grief. I know a brother that'll torch this fucking house for five hundred dollars."

They'd been standing in the drive, Duffy staring at the front door as they talked. "Stay in touch with the guy. It may come to that."

"Hell, he ain't goin' no place."

"We might as well go in and get this over with," said Duffy.

Duffy opened the door, and directly across the room, with his back to him, was Jert, talking to two cops, both holding notepads and writing as he talked. Jert turned at the sound of the opening door, looked at Duffy, blushed violently, and turned back to the cops. Felix sat on the couch and damn if he didn't look as if he was blushing too. What was all this blushing about? Duffy wondered. Tish wasn't there; probably in the bathroom or somewhere in the back of the house.

Tump came in behind Duffy and walked directly across the

room to Jert and, just as one jock will do to another as a matter of course, gave him a hard slap in the ass, saying at the same time: "What's coming down, man?"

Jert screamed and lunged forward, nearly knocking one of the cops off his feet.

"Goddam, Jert," said Tump, "is your dirt track hanging hemorrhoids?"

"You . . . startled me. It's been hell tonight. What are *you* doing here anyway?"

"We're conducting an investigation, sir," said one of the cops. "If you would . . ."

Tish came running from the hallway into the room, her mouth open, her eyes wide. She saw Duffy and stopped. "Thank God. I thought he'd come back or . . ." She stopped when she saw Tump. "Who are you?"

"Tump Walker. I'm the guy that broke your husband's tooth." He looked at Jert. "And I'm suing Duffy for a million dollars, right, Jert?"

"Listen, Tump, I . . ."

"You watch your mouth when you got Tump in it. Don't talk shit with my name," Tump said, and Duffy could hear the coke cooking in his voice.

"Mr. Walker, you back off and keep your *own* mouth shut," said the cop. "I told you we're conducting an investigation here."

"Right you are, officer. Right you are. Old Jert's O.K., but he needs to be straightened out now and then."

One of the cops pointed at Tump, almost touching him on the chest. "Was he as big as this one?"

"Not that big, for God's sake," Jert said.

"This one?" said Tump. "What *one?*"

The cop looked at his notepad. "Male, black, over six feet, very muscular."

Tump's face was tight. "Oh, you mean another nigger."

"I'm only telling you what Mr. McPhester reported. Not a very good make though. Stocking over face."

"Us niggers be heavy into stockings over our faces doing houses and Seven Elevens."

"I don't guess any of you would like to tell me what the hell's going on?" Duffy said.

"Are you Mr. Deeter?" The cop glanced at his notepad. "Mr. Duffy Deeter?"

"That's who I am."

"I can tell you what we have so far."

What they had so far was a marvel to hear. Duffy loved it. Every goddam body in the house was lying, including poor Felix.

"Now, let me see if I understand all this," said Duffy. "Jert, you and Tish were out here in the living room discussing . . ." He looked from one to the other. ". . . business."

"That's right," Jert said, not meeting his eyes.

"And Felix is already in bed? At this hour? Son, have you finally taken you old daddy's advice and stopped watching TV? No TV tonight, huh?"

Felix didn't answer. He was staring at Tump.

"I told you he was in bed, Duffy," said Tish. "Don't be difficult. I'm about at my wits' end."

"I'm just trying to understand. Somebody forced the lock on one of the sliding doors, the TV was off, and you didn't hear him? What the hell were the two of you doing—shouting at each other?"

"We're as much in the dark as you are about this, Duffy," said Jert.

"You were in the dark?" Duffy said, enjoying himself. Might as well play with them. "Why in God's name were the two of you in the dark?"

"It's an expression," Tish said.

"Only an expression, in the dark is," said Jert.

"Sorry," said Duffy, "but this is really weird. I just don't seem to get the picture."

"We were concentrating on what we were doing," said Tish, "and we didn't hear him enter."

"On what you were doing?" said Duffy. He was going to make it just as hard on them as he could.

"*Saying*. Concentrating on what we were saying," Jert said.

"Times *have* been difficult, Duffy," said Tish.

"And that's what we were talking about, how difficult the difficult times have been," said Jert.

Jert was rattled and Duffy was loving it.

"This is not getting us anywhere," said one of the cops. "We need to proceed."

"All right, never mind that you didn't hear him," Duffy said. "What did he do after he was in the room with you?"

"Robbed'm," said Felix. Duffy glanced over at his son. The little bastard was smiling, really grinning. Was he enjoying this as much as Duffy was?

"Took Mr. McPhester's Rolex watch," said one of the cops. Jert didn't wear or own a Rolex watch. He must have reported that to the cops before Tish freaked and called Duffy and told him to come over. Once it was on the theft report, Jert couldn't very well take it back, say it was a mistake. Duffy cut his eyes back to Jert and almost imperceptibly began to shake his head. "And then his wallet, and finally his diamond ring." Jert didn't wear a diamond ring either, and Duffy shook his head harder. Jert didn't own a diamond ring, but Tish did. It had cost him an arm and a leg, and she still had the goddam thing on.

"I see you still got your ring, Tish," Duffy said.

"That's when he hit me with the pistol the first time, and I kind of bowed up at that." Jert pushed his hair off his forehead and showed the tape covering two places at his hairline. The board at the front of the water bed had done a job on him when he butted it.

"We think he was scared off at that point in time," said a cop, "and he made a run for it."

"Totally unfuckingbelievable," said Duffy.

"What?" demanded Jert, and Duffy saw something flash in his face. Was it the angry realization that he had been totally suckered?

"Here in the early part of the evening, lights on, two cars in the driveway, and some guy forces a lock and walks in on you like this. That's unbelievable. Don't you think it's unbelievable, Tump?" But Tump didn't answer, slumping there on the couch beside Felix, sweating under his coke rush, and probably wondering how soon he was going to be able to get out of there and get another line.

"Are you *the* Tump Walker?" Felix asked. "The man that totes the pig?"

Duffy wouldn't have been any more surprised by Felix saying *tote the pig* instead of *carry the ball* if Felix had said it in Greek instead of in English.

Tump winked at the boy. "I don't do nothing if I don't tote the pig."

"Will you sign my football?" asked Felix.

Tump's wide beautiful hand dropped on Felix's round shoulder. "Son, I'd love to sign your ball."

Duffy did not know Felix had a football. He had never thought to ask him. Maybe television was good for something after all.

Felix bounded off the couch and down the hall toward his room. Tish walked over and stood in front of Tump with one hand on her beautiful hip, the hip cocked to one side to curve her body into a lovely question mark. "You play professional football, Mr. Walker." It was a statement.

"Tump, just Tump," he said. But he neither confirmed nor denied the statement. He only sat watching her, his eyes shining and hooded under his smooth brow. Duffy watched them. They seemed balanced there in each other's gaze. Duffy thought Tump must have heard the same thing he, Duffy, had heard in her voice. He didn't recognize it himself, but whatever it was came to him in an image of heat, something that had been tamped down and burning, cooking a long slow time. It was the same quality he'd heard in her voice when she'd been pinned down and working out with Jert. The notion that he didn't know Tish at all began to form in his head.

Felix came in with his football and a Magic Marker. He

handed it to Tump. "Write it big, Tump. God, the Dolphins 'bout give you the franchise to get you out of Philly. Wait'll I show the guys this!"

Duffy felt the floor shift under his feet, or thought he did. Was this Felix, his Felix, talking?

"Mr. Deeter," said one of the cops, who had been staring at his notepad as though adding up a column of figures. "Where were you this evening between eight and . . . say ten o'clock?"

Duffy looked at the cop. Were they onto him? "Is this just general conversation or is there some reason you want to know?"

"Please try to cooperate, Mr. Deeter. We have to make our report as full as possible."

"He was with me," said Tump, handing the ball back to Felix, who stared at the signature that stretched all the way across it. "With me at his old mama's. He went to see her and I went with him."

Jert was incredulous. "You went with him to visit his mother?"

"Mamas are my favorite people in the world. And I like a man that goes to see his mama. You visit your mama, Jert? I bet you hardly do. Did, you wouldn't let your mouth flap on the way you do with other folks' names. Mamas teach a man better than that."

Tish said: "You . . . you met Mother Deeter?"

Duffy had never been able to get Tish not to call her that. His mother hated it, and he had been able to stop Tish from doing it in her presence, but Tish always referred to her that way if the old lady was not around.

"Met her and liked her right off. Reminds me of my own mama."

Jert frowned and hustled his balls, a clear sign that he was either angry or perplexed or both. "How the hell'd you two guys get so tight? You didn't even know each other Sunday."

"We're two of a kind," said Duffy. "We recognized each other, that's all."

"That's it for us," said one of the cops. "It's all we can do tonight. We'll be in touch and increase the patrols on the street for the next few days. But it's not really necessary. They almost never come back."

"If he comes back tonight, he won't find me here," said Tish. "Felix and I are getting out."

The cop said: "Our man secured the door until you can get a locksmith. I'd suggest an alarm system, I mean if I was in your place, a house like this. I hope everything'll be all right, Mr. Deeter." He stopped and looked at Tump. "Sorry I spoke the way I did to you. Only doing my job. We need you down in Miami with the Dolphins . . . and I want to be one of the many folks who's gonna welcome you to the state."

"Ditto that," said the other cop. "That's an affirmative. You do what you do as good as anybody in the world."

Tump smiled and waved them off. "Man can't hear too much of that. You guys take it light."

When the door closed behind the cops, a silence fell in the room. Nobody seemed to know what to say next. Jert touched his forehead gingerly. Felix held his football and stared at Tump's name. Tish busied herself with a cigarette and a lighter.

Tump stood up from the couch and shook his massive shoulders. "Well, Duffy, I don't know what we did here, but whatever it was, it looks like we got to the end of it. If you want to run me back over town, I'll . . ."

"No problem," said Duffy. "Tish and I got a little bit of a problem we're working on here, so I won't be staying either."

Tish said: "Well, I've already said I'm sure as hell not staying here tonight."

"I want to go with Dad," said Felix, in a strange excited voice Duffy couldn't remember hearing before.

"You want to go with your dad?" said Tish.

"And Tump Walker," he said. "I want to go with Tump and Dad."

"I could take Tish to a motel," said Jert.

Duffy stared hard at him, and to his great surprise felt the sudden jolt of something high in his stomach which at first he did not recognize as jealousy. And when he did, he was dumbfounded. He, jealous? But there it was. He made himself hold the hard stare.

"You know, uh, take, uh, see her to a motel nearby," said Jert, stumbling badly, "and, uh, then we'll just take it from there tomorrow."

"Can I come with ycu and Tump, Dad, can I?"

Duffy didn't answer. He was looking at Tish, watching the delicious curve of her ass, thinking about the sounds he'd heard her make with Jert. Surely, these were confusing times.

"Bring the boy, Duffy," Tump said. "It's been too long since I was around a young buck like this."

"Under the circumstances," said Jert, "it might not be a bad idea, Tish. A good quiet night's sleep would do you a world of good."

Duffy thought: Even after having your balls squeezed and hit twice in the ass with a paddle and a busted head, you fat bastard, do you still want to hose her some more tonight?

But instead of the thought bringing rage with it and a desire to fight, it only caused a great sorrow, heavy and palpable as a stone, to settle in him.

14   A full moon flooded the football field in the deep center of the enormous stadium with a golden light that was a brilliant shimmering of the air. Marvella, a cheerleader in high school, was leading the empty stands with cartwheels and splits and chants. She did a back flip, and then shot straight into the air, screaming: "Two bits, four bits, six bits, a dollar, everybody for Tump, stand up and holler."

And from under the far goalpost, Tump, a dark floating shadow against the grass, sprinted forty yards before slowing and jogging back to do it all over again.

Felix, standing on the sideline with a stopwatch in his hand, shouted: "Four-six, Tump. Four-six." Tump jogged by and turned his head toward the boy and showed his gleaming teeth in an easy smile. The smile seemed to snap something in the boy. He pumped up and down on his thick little legs and screamed: "Show me a four-four, Tump. Just one. A four-four. Do it! Do it!"

Marvella whirled and spun, endlessly urging the empty stands to support the effort on the field. Duffy, sitting cross-legged in the grass, breathing heavily, could only watch her and wonder how long she could keep it up. Coke was part of it, but Jesus, she flipped and split and leaped in a way that didn't seem human, as though she were some mechanical contrivance. Tump ran wind sprints in the same way. And fat Felix, who usually nodded out over cookies and milk every night about eleven, was in an absolute frenzy of energy here at two o'clock in the morning.

Only Duffy himself was done in and he knew it. He'd tried to run with Tump, but he simply didn't have the speed for forty yards, and besides that, to his great surprise, the four sprints he did attempt had exhausted him. No question, things were definitely fucked up. Going the wrong way. He'd made a wrong turn somewhere.

Tump blew past, a blurred shadow that did not seem to touch the ground.

Felix screamed. It was a sound he might have made if his hand had just been caught in a meat grinder. Then he yelled: "Four-four! A *goddam* four-four."

Duffy had never heard his son curse before. Tump trotted back and stopped beside Felix. Felix tossed him his football, which Tump one-handed, then he said: "Son, there's a bunch of folks that can do forty yards in four-four."

Which is precisely what Tump had said earlier when they were back in his condominium. It was the statement that had eventually led them here to the stadium in the middle of the night.

On the way back over to Marvella's so Tump could pick up the bag of coke, he had suggested that they all go over to his place. "We can slide over to my condo," he said. "Lot of room. No problem."

"Yeah," screamed Felix in Duffy's ear, "let's slide over to Tump's condo."

"What are you doing with a place in Gainesville?" asked Duffy.

"I don't own it, man. It's a loaner."

"A loaner?"

"Part of the deal."

"Which deal are we talking about?"

"A piece of a beer distributorship. That's how I got up with McPhester to start with. You don't think I hang out with jacklegs like that unless there's something coming down I need'm for, do you? The beer thing came as part of the Dolphin trade. I need a lawyer and my agent— Hey, is this boring you? It's just boring the shit out of me. Could we get over to my place and cool out?" He turned to look at Felix, who was standing directly behind him. "What about it, cowboy? Don't you think we need to cool out?"

Felix, in a tight, serious little voice, said: "I know *I* need to cool out."

Duffy stared straight ahead and wondered at this stranger Felix was turning into.

Marvella could not believe the place Tump lived in. It *was* huge. And everything was done in white, even the rugs. The condominium took up an entire floor of the building.

"Godamighty, Tump," said Marvella, "you could stable horses in this place."

Tump looked around at the living room as though seeing it for the first time.

"Never thought of it just like that. But, yeah, we could stable horses in here."

Duffy looked at Marvella with a loving, quiet loathing. Stable horses in the living room? Right. Sure. Good Alabama girl she was and good Alabama girl she would remain. She was pure, perfect of her kind. It was good to know that there were some things pure and perfect in the world. Maybe that was why he had kept her around. "I've got to eat," said Tump. "I need to get on the outside of about five pounds of carbos."

"Eat?" said Marvella. "God, are you hungry after all that"— she glanced at Felix but went ahead and said it—"coke?"

"Hungry's got nothing to do with it, sweetheart. I've got to feed the machine. The machine's all I got and I can't slight it just because I'm goofing. I'm gonna get on the horn and order up five or six pizzas."

108

"All *right*, Tump!" cried Felix. "I could eat some pizza. Let's feed the old machine!"

"Supreme mothers. Everything. Pepperoni, sausage, mushrooms, the whole nine yards. Including anchovies. Anchovies all right with you, Felix?"

"Tump," said Felix, dead serious now, "I eat anything."

Tump thought it was funny as hell. Laughing, he said, "I may eat the mothering cartons they come in, Buckshot."

"Me too," said Felix. "Let's you and me eat the pizzas and then turn right around and eat the cartons."

Tump looked at Duffy and Marvella. "Anybody against anchovies?"

"It'll be a long time before I think about food again," she said. "I don't know how you can blow dust and eat."

"How the hell you think I stay this big? Ain't no calories in crank."

"Do you eat that shit, Tump?" asked Duffy. "Do you really eat it?"

"Run that by again, Duff," said Tump.

"What?" Duffy was confused. Coke did funny things to his head. He was going to have to go down to his Winnebago and get his bottle of Jack Daniel's.

Marvella said, "Say it again, Hardrock. Tump and I missed a transition." And then she giggled.

"There's enough sodium and grease in a pizza to kill a mule," Duffy said.

"But not a nigger," said Tump. "Specially one that"—and he looked at Felix and winked—"totes the pig. Sodium keeps me from cramping. And grease is full of get-go."

"Grease is full of get-go," murmured Felix, speaking to himself, musing on the phrase, which he liked very much. It justified something in his life. He could not have said it, but he knew it. "Full of the old get-go," he almost whispered.

Tump picked up the telephone and ordered five pizzas. "Yeah," he said. "Yeah, supreme mothers."

Duffy went down to his Winnebago and got his bottle of Jack

Daniel's and Marvella chopped out some lines of coke on a mirror. In a very short time, during which little was said except for Felix chattering on about the National Football League, its players and teams and coaches and schedules and past Super Bowls, they were all sitting on the deep pile carpet of the living room, Tump and Felix tearing at huge chunks of pizza while Duffy and Marvella sat in the lotus position, Duffy taking short hits from his bottle and Marvella leaning to the mirror for brief toots of coke.

Duffy glanced at the pizza and looked as though he smelled something rotten. "I don't see how a world-class athlete would allow himself to eat that swill."

Tump only smiled. "There's swill and there's swill, my man. I don't think Herschel Walker even ate at the training table when he played at Georgia. Herschel *lives* off hamburgers. He goes out and eats five hamburgers and his arms get an inch bigger and a half second comes off his forty. You dig? When I was growing up I ate anything that came to hand and was glad to get it. Still do. I eat *anything*."

Felix, ravaging a slice of pizza, fixed Tump with a steady eye and said, "You and me are a lot alike."

"I *know* that's right," said Tump. "Knew it when I saw you. 'Cause you know what? When I was your age, I was built like you. First thing I thought of when I saw you. Hell, boy, you'll probably grow up to tote the pig yourself."

Felix stopped chewing and put his slice of pizza down. He looked over at his father and then back at Tump. "Well, I have thought about it."

It was all too much for Duffy. Marvella had slipped out of lotus position, which he had made her assume in the first place, and he told her to take it up again. She had been through this hundreds of times before and did what he told her to do without complaint.

But holding the rolled dollar bill lightly between thumb and forefinger, she did ask, "You haven't said anything about the trip. When we going on the trip?"

"I think we're on it," said Duffy. "Yes, we are definitely on the trip. It is not the trip I planned, but then the absence of a plan is also some plan."

Tump cut his eyes toward Duffy but did not say anything.

Duffy closed his eyes and said: "We are thinking now of the great One, trying to avoid avidya, the ignorance and delusion that come from the belief that the self and the world are separate." In the light filtering through his lashes he saw Marvella's blurred form bend to the mirror, and he heard the air rush in her nostril as she sucked up a line of coke. "Avidya keeps us from bodhi, which is enlightenment, the only enlightenment." He knew she was not paying him the slightest attention, never had when he had tried to bring her to Zen. It had never bothered him before. Now he felt the fool. And worse, he didn't have the dimmest notion why he was doing what he was doing. He longed for a drink out of his whiskey bottle, but he wouldn't stop. He wouldn't *let* himself stop. "Buddha-nature is held tightly in the four vows every Buddhist recites morning and evening, trying to keep them constantly in mind, constantly before him."

Tump's voice broke over his last word. "Say, Duff?" Duffy did not open his eyes, did not turn his head. "Duffy. Hey, come on, looka here." Duffy opened his eyes and looked at Tump, who was chewing slowly, waving a slice of pizza, dripping with strings of cheese, in the air. "Say, you ain't into that suckananda fuckananda scam, are you? You know, those shaved-down assholes with the pigtails and the robes who try to nickel and dime you to death at the airport."

"You don't know what you're saying, Tump," said Duffy. "What those people do, their way of life, is based on an ancient and honorable—religious, if you want to say that—book called the Bhagavad-Gita."

"I already told you I didn't just go practice, I went to class. You're not going to tell me that it says somewhere in the book that those suckers oughta be jacking around with folks in airports."

111

"I never said that, Tump. I could talk to you about vows of poverty, but I won't."

"No, don't. Me and my people didn't have to take no *vow* to be poor. It just came as part of the package. But, hey, go on with what you doing. Me and Felix are getting along just fine. This is righteous pizza. Go on and give us the four vows every Buddhist recites every morning and evening. Lighten up, Duff. I'm sorry I broke in on you. And stop frowning, man. You die that way, you'll be ugly in the casket."

Duffy had not realized he was frowning. He reached for his bottle and took a long drink. He started to recite the vows by rote. They meant nothing to him. He rambled on about samsara, the wheel of Birth and Death, and about the relationship between Nirvana and Karma, but again he was on automatic pilot. He might as well have been reciting a grocery list for all the words meant to him. What he was actually thinking about was the corpses he carried in his head to keep fucking, his light bicycle and heavy chain, the whiplash trial he had lost because the lady's neck as well as the wreck had vanished in the courtroom, and then he became acutely aware of his hand resting on the whiskey bottle while he recited holy vows, and of Tump— a great athlete—chewing away on chunk after chunk of pizza, all the while stopping now and again to do a line of coke off Marvella's mirror, and, finally, of Tish—wherein his voice slowed and finally stopped in midsentence. Tish, Jesus, Tish: her voice behind the sliding glass door and under Jert, the insolent, hot cock of her hip when she met Tump.

Duffy suddenly stood out of the lotus position and said in a strangled voice: "We've got to stop this."

"I know that's right," said Tump, sucking his teeth.

"I do too," said Felix, finishing the last bit of crust left in one of the cartons.

Tump looked at the boy and put his hand on his shoulder. "Dammit, son, that was some serious eating. You keep eating like that and you're gonna knock a lot of dicks in the dirt before you're through."

"By God, I like serious eating, I do," said Felix.

Tump looked at Duffy, who had not moved. "You got something on your mind, Duffy?"

Duffy thought again about just blurting it all out as he had thought about doing earlier, but he answered, "No, nothing."

Tump stood, uncoiling off the floor like a spring. "Good, 'cause I do. I feel like running. Want to run some wind sprints, Duffy, do some forties?"

Felix thrashed on the floor and finally got to his feet, his face flushed. "Hot damn! Now we got it! Run the old forties!"

"Run after eating all that pizza?" said Duffy.

"Sure."

"That's crazy. All that food in your stomach and you're going to sprint? You'll die if you run after eating all that."

"Duffy, you don't take a trip and then put fuel in your car. You put in the fuel and then take the trip. I have to think of my body as a machine or I couldn't compete. When I'm working out or playing, I have this image of a little man sitting in my skull just above the eyes and in front of him is a control panel and, man, that panel is full of different-colored lights and switches and a little speaker that sends messages from all over my body."

"Weird," said Marvella.

"Probably," Tump said. "But I take a lick on the field and the message comes through the speaker to the little man in my head: *'Right knee damage! Right knee going out!'* The little man checks his control panel, I mean I can *see* him checking it, and he sends back the instructions and the command: *'No damage in right knee. Repeat, no damage! Take it back to full speed!'* And I do. I've had that little man with me since I was . . . since I was . . ." He looked at Felix. ". . . since I was his age."

Felix's soft little body undulated with pleasure. "I'm gonna get me one of them. I could use a little man in my head." He glanced at Duffy. "I could use him for a whole lot of things sometimes."

Duffy liked the notion himself. He didn't have a little man, and didn't intend to get one. But he did have, by God, enthusiasm.

Tump asked, "Can we get into the stadium at the university? I'd just as soon have an even surface to run on."

"No problem getting in," said Duffy. "But it'd be easier to go to the track."

Marvella's face flushed and her voice was almost a squeal when she spoke. "The stadium. Oh, let's go to the stadium. I'll do my cheers, bring the crowd to its feet."

Strung and warped at the same time, thought Duffy. But what he said was: "There is no crowd, Marvella. None. Nobody."

Her pinned eyes swung to hold on his, her face tight and serious. "The absence of a crowd is also some crowd."

"Lay back off saying shit like that," said Tump. "It bothers me."

"Did you know," she asked Tump, "that while I was in high school I went to the Dixie National Baton Twirling Institute every single summer."

"No," said Tump. "I didn't know that."

"Did, though," said Marvella. "When I was there the director of the Institute was Don Sartell. He was called Mr. Baton, you know." Babbling, she paused to draw a quick shallow breath. "Course I don't have my baton. But I can cheer. Boy, you wait till you see me cheer. The twirling institute was on the campus of Ole Miss. That's not in Alabama, where I come from. It's in Jackson, Mississippi. You know where that is?"

"Sure he does," said Felix. Again, he went very serious, his smooth little face tightening in a frown. "Everybody in the whole world—except maybe five or six people—knows that Tump Walker was born in Tupelo, Mississippi, but played his college ball at Florida A & M." He looked at Tump. "Too bad you were too late for Coach Jake Gaither." He looked back at Marvella. "A legend is all Jake Gaither was. Everybody knew he was better than Coach Bear Bryant. Even the Bear knew it. Coach Gaither just happened to be at a littler school."

Duffy could only stare at his son. Who was this stranger?

"Damn, cowboy, I may show you a four-four," Tump said. "And you can hold the stopwatch. There's a moon out tonight, big moon. Bring your football. You may have to go long for a couple."

"You still got four-four speed?" Felix asked the question as though he were asking if there was a God.

"Sometimes," said Tump. "I feel good tonight, feel a*gile*, mob*ile* and host*ile*." He smiled.

"There!" cried Felix. "That's Coach Jake Gaither. That's his words. That's the way he told his players they had to be."

"He also told'm if they weren't, he'd break their plate," said Tump.

"Break their plate?" said Duffy.

Felix looked at his father as though he were a hopeless imbecile. "It means they wouldn't be able to eat at the training table. And if they couldn't do that, they'd have to buy their own food."

"And for a poor boy on a football scholarship," said Tump, "that ain't good."

"Right," said Felix.

"You'd like my mother," said Duffy. "She's full of phrases like that, talks in a kind of code."

Tump looked at Duffy a long moment. "I probably would like her. But not for that. I just like mamas." He cut his eyes toward Felix. "I like daddies too, but they ain't important as mamas."

"I never thought they were, either," said Marvella.

Duffy didn't like that, especially said in front of Felix. Although his instant reaction was to think it was probably true. "That's a hell of a thing to say."

"Only speaking from experience, Duffy," Tump said.

"Me, too," said Marvella.

Duffy thought of his own mother keeping the house and their lives together while his strange father roared about on secret and dangerous missions and made machine-gun noises over the glued-together replicas of World War II aircraft. It occurred to

115

him that he had done precious little to hold his own family together. It was a thought that didn't please him and he shook it off. He was not going to get caught comparing lives. The world began again, brand-new, with every life and ended with every death. There were as many worlds as there were people, and he had done the best he could with his. Fuck it, he wasn't going to beat on himself about it. Leave that to the weak sticks of the world. If he knew anything, he knew enough to forgive himself. He was not guilty of his life; it was something that happened to him. He thought he'd probably read that somewhere. But it was not important if he had. What was important was that he believed it.

"Let's see if we can move this circus somewhere else," said Duffy, in a voice too loud and too sudden.

Felix pitched Tump his football. "Do you *really* still have four-four speed in the forty?"

Tump said: "Son, there's a bunch of folks that can do forty yards in four-four."

And that was the line, Tump's statement, that had brought them here to the stadium under a full, brilliant moon for Tump to run sprints and Marvella to cheer her heart out in front of empty stands while Duffy sat in the grass and watched.

"All right, go out twenty yards," said Tump. He had a hand on each of Felix's shoulders, bending down so that their heads almost touched. "Angle right and look over your shoulder. The ball will be there when you look, so look hard. Forget everything else and look for the ball. We doing a timing pass. I'm throwing to a spot, so the ball'll be in the air before you ever look. But be where you're supposed to be and this'll work."

"I'll be there, Tump."

"Remember, we're down three points. There's eight seconds left and no time-outs. Out of field goal range to put it into overtime. No sideline patterns. We're still on our own thirty. It's all on you, Felix."

"A piece of cake," said Felix and there was no mistaking that the confidence in his voice was genuine.

Tump and Felix clapped their hands in unison as they broke the huddle, and Felix went to hunker over the ball. Tump dropped into a half squat so that his hands were between Felix's fat thighs to receive the ball. On the sideline, Duffy was no longer sitting. Tump talking to Felix about their situation on the field, the desperate position they were in, had brought him to his feet. The edge of competition quickened in his blood. And Felix! Jesus, Felix was going to do it.

Felix churned straight ahead when he hiked the ball. Tump waited, then lofted the pass with a feather touch. At the second hash mark, Felix cut right and held out his short fat little arms and the ball dropped right into them. He put his head down, and with the cheeks of his ass gobbling the seat of his trousers, ran seventy yards to the end zone, where he spiked the ball, and held his soft-knuckled fists over his head.

Tump ran to congratulate him, and Marvella spun and split on the sidelines. Duffy could only stand in an icy sweat with a strange knot of admiration swelling in his throat.

15

Duffy woke up in a strange bed, not knowing where he was. He looked at his watch. Eleven-thirty. Sunlight poured through the parted curtain. He heard a door close and presently Tump walked by the open door of Duffy's room. He was naked except for a towel wrapped around his lean hips, and water dripped off him as he paused. He pointed a forefinger and cocked his thumb.

"Pow," he said, smiling. "I just zapped you of all guilt for the next year." Then he laughed as though he'd just heard the funniest joke in the world. "Been in the Jacuzzi. You oughta try it. You look like shit."

After Tump walked past the doorway and on down the hall, Felix appeared as if by magic. He had a towel wrapped around his hips and water ran in the creases of his fat. "Been in the Jacuzzi," he said. "You oughta try it." When he paused as if to say something else, Duffy wondered if his son was going to tell him he looked like shit. It would not have surprised him if he had, but Felix only pointed his forefinger, cocked his thumb and said, "Pow." And when he laughed, the laugh sounded not like an imitation of Tump's but genuine and deeply felt.

Duffy closed his eyes and tried not to think. He had slept soundly but he was still exhausted. And as he remembered the night before, he got even more tired. A heaviness settled in his bones as he thought of Marvella springing, leaping and lunging about in front of the empty stadium seats while Tump ran sprint after sprint up and down the darkened football field.

When it was finally over, Felix—wildly exuberant over his own touchdown—had bounded up the steps of the Winnebago with a nimbleness that Duffy had never seen in him before. Instead of going back to Marvella's, they had come here to Tump's condominium, although Duffy could not remember exactly why. Maybe because it had more room, more beds. Duffy had whipped the Winnebago through the darkened streets and tried not to think of the things he was finding out about his son.

Behind him Marvella was singing at the top of her lungs:

> Give a cheer, give a shout,
> For the girls who dish it out
> In the cellars of old Jackson High.
>
> They are brave, they are bold,
> For the fifteen inches they can hold
> In the cellars of old Jackson High.
>
> It's hi, hi, hee
> And to hell with Robert E. Lee
> The girls over there can't even peeeeeee.

"Damn, girl," said Tump. "Turn that down about two notches."

"Don't worry about a thing," said Marvella. "Everything's under control. I've got Seconal, Tuinal and Nembutal to get us down off this mountain and help us sleep."

"Darling, Tump Walker don't ever need anything to sleep."

"Don't shit a shitter, Tumps. No way you could close it down after all that dust."

"Little girl, right up my left nostril is a switch. I just slip my little finger up there and flip it. I'm asleep."

"You're a wonder," Marvella giggled. "A goddam wonder."

"Hey, Tump," said Felix. "We're not going to *bed*, are we?"

"That's where we going, Buckshot."

"Aw, Tump, I don't want to go to bed. I'm not sleepy. I'm not even tired. Maybe we could . . . I don't know. We could . . ."

"We could sleep. We could and we are. You want to tote the pig? All right, three things then. The right sleep. The right food. The right exercise. All three. Not two. Not one. Three, all *three*. You gotta park the machine."

Felix came back in instant agreement: "Park the machine. Right! Park the ole *machine*."

It was only what Duffy had said to him about ten thousand times before. And ten thousand times before, Duffy told himself he might as well have been talking to a brick. He held the steering wheel as a drowning man holds the gunwale of a lifeboat. All the while, in the back, Marvella gave rousing football cheers. Duffy could not stand it and flipped a switch and a roar of voices stopped her cold. Hitler was boiling the blood of a vast audience of Germans.

"The fucking man's done laid Hitler on us," said Tump.

Duffy turned his head briefly and tried to show Tump a smile. "Hell of a speaker, right?"

Tump said, "Why'd you turn that on, Duff?"

"Because Hitler took what he got by main strength." Duffy had had no idea he was going to say what he said.

"Kill that motherfucker, man," said Tump. "Turn it off."

Duffy hit the switch and the tape stopped. Hitler's voice had gone up his spine like a jolt of electricity. He felt a little better; not much, but a little.

"Didn't mean to get tight," said Tump, "but this is the wrong time of night to listen to a fucking lunatic."

"Lunacy is also a kind of sanity," said Duffy. "Lunacy makes up its own rules just like sanity does." Duffy raised his whiskey bottle and took a drink.

"Pass that," said Tump.

So far as Duffy knew, Tump had not had a drink tonight, but now he took the bottle and raised it to Duffy in a toast. "Fuckananda suckananda," he said.

Marvella went back to cheering, and when they got to Tump's she dropped three bootleg Quaaludes and went down for the count on the couch. Duffy carried her back to a room and dumped her on a bed. She was so knocked out by cheering and dope that she looked as if she had fallen from a great height, her head and legs twisting off at strange angles. Duffy thought she looked very much as if she were dead, and he said in a soft lugubrious voice, just the sort he hated most, being as it was full of self-pity: "What is all this shit with corpses?"

On the way back down the hall, he passed a room with twin beds. Tump, stripped out of his running shorts, lay naked and snoring softly on one of them. Felix lay on the other. He had not even managed to take off his shoes, and lay fully clothed, breathing with a sound that an aging English bulldog might have made. Or at least that was the way it had always seemed to Duffy since Felix started snoring, shortly after his third birthday. He went into the room and touched his boy's hair, still damp from his touchdown run, and he wanted to say something, but he didn't know what to say. He could feel the words bouncing around at the back of his tongue in a kind of garbled strangle. But nothing came, and he went back out to the couch and opened the fresh bottle of Jack Daniel's that he'd brought up with him from the Winnebago.

But the longer and more deeply he drank of the bottle, the more convinced he became that the whiskey was not going to take. He was sober as a stone and for all the good the bottle was doing him he might as well have been drinking ice water. And he wasn't even surprised. He knew the reason. His mind had seized upon Tish and Jert and the motel they were laid up in. He knew the place, could see their cars parked side by side in the macadam lot under the bright light of the moon. It would be the Gainesville Hilton, where Tish always reserved rooms for her relatives when they came to town, the same place where she and Duffy and Felix had stayed while their house was being repainted after smoke damage. He felt the images anchored in his heart: the two cars parked sweetly side by side in the moonlight, Tish and Jert lying sweatily side by side, with maybe light from the same moon slanting across the tossed covers and their damp flesh.

He got up from the couch and went into the bathroom, where he stood looking in the mirror. He watched himself lift the bottle and take a drink. "You are as confused as a ten-dick dog," he said. "And when confused, the thing to do is act. Action is all. Well, most times." He paused a moment and thought about it. "Fuck most times. It *always* is at four o'clock in the morning. Four o'clock in the morning is no time for thought. Thoughts become poisonous in the dark hours of morning." He watched his face a moment, thinking that what he'd said made sense.

He left the bathroom and went down to his Winnebago, taking the whiskey bottle in his hand. When he pulled into the Gainesville Hilton's parking lot, he had a bittersweet shock of recognition as though he had seen the two cars parked next to one another before, sitting on the dark macadam under the declining moon now touching the treeline at the far horizon. Which of course is how he had imagined them back in the living room of Tump's condominium. He pulled in behind them and got out. It was as though the sight of them had released the alcohol in his blood, sending a hot flush up from his chest which came to settle behind his eyes. The taste of sour corn flooded his mouth and in a moment he was pleasantly drunk. He set his bottle on top of Tish's car and turned to regard Jert's red Corvette, slowly, almost bemused, and in the first wash of light-headedness his mother's madly sane little voice spoke to him, saying one of the things she liked to say the most: "Don't worry. What comes next always comes next. You don't even have to think about it." And he didn't. The answer to what he was to do next was in the metal whiplash aerial of Jert's car, rising out of the fender in front of the windshield in a long arc that ended at the rear bumper.

Duffy longed to have it whistling over his head as soon as he saw it, even before he struck it with the flat of his palm and it came off in his hand. And God, it did feel not just good but *right*, better than he'd even thought it would, when he brought the limber rod of steel down over the hood of the car. He worked steadily, unhurriedly, as though he might be doing an exercise instead of whipping a car. A satisfying sting ran in his hand and arm every time he struck. Sweat ran on his face. The moon touched the trees and then started to descend into them. The only sound anywhere was the crack of metal on metal in the still air over the deserted parking lot.

"Yo, Duffy! You want'm up or over?"

Duffy's eyes jerked open. His face was damp. He could feel the stinging in his hand and hear the sharp crack of metal on metal. Confused, he struggled up from the bed. "Yeah! Right! What?"

"Two ways," Tump called. "Up or over?"

Duffy pulled on his clothes and went barefoot through the living room to the kitchen. As he went through the living room he saw his shoes by the couch where he'd left them the night before, and beside them the whiskey bottle, left open and untouched. When he'd come back from the Hilton parking lot, he'd had no thought of drinking more, only of sleep. He had not dreamed.

In the kitchen, Tump and Felix were still wearing towels wrapped around their hips, Tump standing at the stove, a spatula in his hand, and Felix sitting on a low stool, his little cock poking through the towel looking directly at Duffy, and for that matter, directly at Marvella had she chosen to lift her head out of her hands where she sat with her elbows on a table. Marvella's hair was matted. Her skin looked as if she had just thrown up or as if she might be going to.

"Marvella, you look full of death," said Duffy.

"And you sound full of shit," she said. She didn't look up.

That was not like her, but Duffy only smiled. He felt better now that he was up.

"Come on, Duff," said Tump. "You holding up a man at work."

"What?" said Duffy.

Felix said, "You gotta order'm to get'm."

123

"Get what?"

"For Christ sake, Dad," said Felix. "Eggs. Remember eggs, food? Come out of the woods and get in the ball game. We tryin' to feed the old machine."

Something here was beginning to spoil Duffy's morning. And he didn't want it spoiled. He stared at his son.

"Felix, put your cock back in the towel."

"I've seen a cock before," said Marvella. "Leave the kid alone and get on with the goddam food. All this talk about eating is making my eyeballs hot."

"Ain't talk making your eyeballs hot, sweetheart," said Tump.

"I know what'll cool'm off," said Marvella.

"You already ate it all," said Tump.

"I didn't eat the stash at my place," she said.

"I didn't eat *anything* yet," said Felix.

He had not put his cock back behind the towel. If anything, thought Duffy, he was showing a little of his balls now too. Well, these were strange times.

Tump winked at Felix. "Tell it straight, my man. Your daddy's stunned, so you and me are going to let him be. Tump's going to cook it up and put it out."

"Take it an' run, Biggun," said Felix, rocking to one side and farting briefly. "I need grease bad."

"You might get into grease later," said Tump. "This morning it's protein and carbs."

"Anything I can chew up," said the boy.

"Do it! Do it and quit talking about it," cried Marvella in a tight voice on the edge of hysteria.

And Tump did it. He opened the refrigerator, took out thick sirloin steaks, and threw them on a flame broiler. Then he spooned dollops of butter on a wide griddle where half a dozen eggs were lined up in a narrow trough.

Duffy, feeling a stir in his guts, said, "Me, too, Tump." Then: "I'll eat mine however you're doing yours." He glanced at his son. "And Felix's."

Tump took out another dozen eggs. Through the open door,

Duffy saw melons and peaches, all manner of fruit, and rounds of cheese and loaves of uncut bread.

"I can't believe you ate that shit last night," said Duffy, "with all this great stuff in the kitchen."

Tump shrugged. "Came with the place. Besides, last night I didn't feel like nothing but pizza. This morning my stomach's somebody else." He was chopping fruit into an enormous bowl. "I'm always the same guy, but my stomach's got a mind of its own."

Felix slapped himself over his navel. "Tump, I am just like you."

16

"For Christ's sake, hurry, will you," said Marvella.

Duffy drove the Winnebago through the midday streets of Gainesville at a leisurely pace. He was enjoying Marvella's discomfort, but that gave him no pleasure because he knew she was hurting, and he didn't like to think that he enjoyed someone else's pain. But he knew he did.

"I need a line," she said.

"I don't see why I couldn't stay with Tump," said Felix from where he stood behind Duffy.

"He's got things to do, son," said Duffy. "I think you know that."

"I think I could do without the conversation until I get a line," said Marvella. "The conversation is twisting me."

"You ought to cool out," said Duffy. "Even Tump told you you ought to try to cool out."

"I could also live the rest of my life quite nicely, thank you, without ever being told to cool out again." She lit a cigarette and spoke through a cloud of smoke. "Could I just not hear it again until I get home?"

"Right," said Duffy. Her skin was dead gray and covered with a thin shine of sweat that he knew would be cold to the touch. There was definitely something wrong with the girl. But what did that say about him? He kept her, didn't he? He shook off the question and tried to fill his head with nothing but blue light, but what he saw lying in the blue light was the corpse of Marvella.

Behind him, Felix clapped a long fart and said, "I hope we get somewhere pretty soon. I think I've got to give dirt."

He'd got that way of talking from Tump, the business of giving dirt. Felix had picked up everything Tump said and repeated it instantly as though it had been his forever. And Duffy felt an absolute pain in his heart that such had never been the case between his son and himself. Duffy could not remember a single time he had ever heard his own voice in Felix's mouth. But until now, it occurred to him, he had never wanted to.

At Marvella's apartment, Felix was the one to see the car first. "Look at that Vette! It's been beat to shit!" Then, after the smallest pause: "It looks like Jert's. It really does, except it's all busted."

And busted it was, sitting there in the glaring sun beside the apartment complex. Duffy turned to look at it as he passed. Jesus, he hadn't thought he'd done that much damage to it. He must have been drunker than he thought. But what in the hell was it doing parked there?

And then, as he stopped, he saw Jert and Tish rushing through the shimmering air toward them. It was Tish who jerked his door open and looked as if she meant to throttle him where he sat behind the wheel, but, no, she was only hysterical, really hysterical this time.

"You've got to do something, Duffy," she cried.

"What's wrong, Mom?" Felix was immediately almost in tears because his mother's face was puffy, swollen maybe from crying, because her eyes were red, and her hair, her perfect hair, was uncombed and matted to her neck with sweat. "Is that Jert's car? How come it's busted?"

"What the hell are you doing here?" demanded Duffy. He tried to sound genuinely mystified and indignant.

Marvella got out, only looking back long enough to shout: "I don't know what the fuck this is, but I can't play this shit right now." Then she actually sprinted toward the stairs to her apartment. Duffy watched her go, and even as his wife was pulling at his shirt and babbling, he couldn't help but admire Marvella's cheerleading legs pumping, her knees high, her tight little ass bouncing in a fetching way.

Felix was pulling at Duffy's other sleeve. "Dad, don't make Mom cry."

"I'm not making her cry, Felix. I don't even know what's going on here."

"You've got to do something," said Tish.

Duffy sighed. He felt as if he was doing all of this pretty well. Even the sigh was a good touch.

"I kind of thought I *was* doing something. I just drove across town for starters. I took care of Felix before that. Now I'm sitting here being pulled on and yelled at."

Jert was standing behind Tish, looking a little lost. He said, "She made me bring her here, Duffy. She wouldn't have it any other way."

"Which other way was there to have it, Jert?"

"I could have taken care of it, Duffy."

"What is it you could have taken care of, Jert?"

"Somebody is after us, for God's sake," said Tish.

"You've got to do something, Dad," said Felix.

"This is madness," said Duffy. "Fucking madness."

"Somebody vandalized my car, Duffy."

"Vandalized, shit," Duffy said. "It looks like somebody took a tire iron to it."

"We figure they whipped it with my aerial."

"Somebody whipped your car with your aerial?"

"That's the way it looks," said Jert.

"While you," said Tish, getting redder in the face, "while you were . . . were . . . Where the hell were you?"

"We were at Tump's place, Mom." Felix was crying now

128

himself. "He's got this wonderful huge ole place and we had a . . . we had fun."

Jert took his belly in both hands and gently massaged it. "I should have *known* that's where you were."

Tish spun on him. "What do you know about this?" She was livid, livid with Duffy and with Jert and with the whole world, probably really livid with her fallen, sweaty hairdo.

"Tish, I'm Tump's lawyer. I arranged for the condo. It's part of the deal."

"I'm sick of deals. To hell with deals. Somebody's after us."

"Ah," said Duffy, "we're back to that. Now why don't we just hold it right there and maybe we can get off the dime."

"Off the dime?" said Tish. "I want off the world. I want protection."

"You want protection from me?" said Duffy.

"Not from you. You're my husband, dammit."

"You're the man, Dad. It's third and long. It's all up to you."

In spite of himself, Duffy liked that. He even let himself hope it might be true.

"It only makes sense," said Jert, "that something is seriously wrong here. Somebody breaks into Tish's . . . your house, robs us, and pistol whips me. We go to the Hilton—that's where Tish wanted to spend the night—and while we were in the room, somebody, no doubt the same somebody, comes and wrecks my car." Duffy could see the moment on Jert's face when he realized the mistake he had made. "I walked Tish up to the room, of course, and she was distraught, so I ordered up a couple of drinks."

"Of course," said Duffy.

"And, hell, it couldn't have been more than an hour when I came down and . . . well, you see the car."

"That would have made it about ten, eleven latest, right?" said Duffy. He pursed his lips and blew a little puff of air. "Damn, you would have thought somebody would have seen it."

"You would've thought so. The point is, though, that now I've got to go take care of some stuff down at the police station."

He pointed to his ruined car. "That's a twenty-five-thousand-dollar investment."

"I know what it cost, Jert," said Duffy.

"Whatever, Tish wants you to take her to the house to get the things she needs to go where she's going."

"I *demand* you take me this instant. You can't seem to comprehend that somebody is after . . . after whoever they're after, and I for one want to be someplace far away when he shows up again."

Duffy said, "I comprehend, I do. But could we go a little light on the demands just now? I don't feel much like responding to a fucking demand."

"Duffy, will you take me, please, and get me out of here?"

Felix said, "You just got the ball, Coach."

"It seems that way, Felix. Get in, Tish."

She didn't even say goodbye to Jert, but left him standing there watching them pull off in the Winnebago.

Felix patted her shoulder. "You'll be all right, Mom."

"This has been the goddamndest night and day of my life."

"You should've been with us, Mom. Tump is probably the greatest . . . I don't even know what, but we had a great time. Pizza, and running forties in the stadium, and steak for breakfast."

"What is this about running in the stadium?"

"We'll tell you about it, Tish. Just take a few deep breaths and try to bring your blood pressure down about forty notches."

"You ever been in a Jacuzzi, Mom? Tump's got the greatest fucking Jacuzzi in the world."

"Watch your language, young man. You're away one night and you come back talking like a sailor."

There, you young shit, thought Duffy, your mother will jack your little ass up. But he thought it with affection.

Tish looked into the rearview mirror and brushed her platinum hair behind her ears. "And, yes, for your information, I have been in a Jacuzzi."

Duffy turned to look at her. She sure as hell had not been

in one with him. But he drove on toward their house without saying anything. When they stopped at the bottom of the drive, Tish didn't want to go in.

"Then what did I bring you here for?" said Duffy.

"Don't you see? I just don't want to. I'm afraid."

"You don't need to be afraid," he said.

"That's easy for you to say."

"Yes," he admitted, "that is easy for me to say."

"Nobody's after *you*."

"Trust me," he said. "Nobody's after you either."

"Come on, Mom," said Felix. "We're with you."

"Something strange has been going on for a very long time," he said, and then regretted saying it.

But she didn't seem to notice. "All right, then," she said. "Let's do it."

"Thatta girl, Mom. Suck it up. We'll take the bigguns one by one and the littluns two by two."

She looked at the boy as if he were a stranger. "What's got into you?"

Felix held her stare and never blinked. "I guess I've just grown up."

She looked at him a moment longer and then got out. But when they entered the house, she only stood in the living room, her gaze lost in the middle distance.

"I don't know where to start," she said.

"Just get some stuff for yourself. And something for Felix."

"But where are we going?" It was almost a wail.

"This is make-it-up-as-we-go time, darlin'," said Duffy. "We'll think of something."

She went into the back room and he could hear her throwing things about. She called something to him about suitcases, but he didn't understand and didn't answer. He made himself a whiskey instead. He sat by Felix on the couch.

"You sure drink a lot of that stuff," said Felix.

"I do, son. At times I do. But I'm going to tell you something. I wouldn't trust a man who could get through this cold sober."

"This? This what?"

"Life, son. A man who could get through it cold sober is either a fool or he isn't paying attention."

"Oh," said Felix, his fine brow breaking in thought. "I guess I'll understand about all that later."

"I expect you will, son. You can count on it." Duffy finished his whiskey and even as the last of it drained into his mouth it came to him that he could not remember ever sitting down and talking with his son this way. This was all something new.

The telephone rang. Tish came rushing down the hall and looked from the ringing telephone to Duffy and back again.

"Are you going to answer that?" asked Duffy.

"Certainly not," she said. "It's them."

Felix got off the couch. "It's only a phone, Mom." He picked it up and gave a cry of joy that sounded curiously like a scream. And then Tish screamed and fell onto the couch, where Duffy caught her in his arms.

"How's the baddest of the bad, my man?" cried Felix. And then: "Good, real good. Sure, he's right here." He turned to Duffy, who was trying to comfort Tish. "It's for you, Dad. Tump."

"What can *he* want?" asked Tish, still near hysteria.

"I'll have to talk to him first before I can find out," said Duffy, taking the phone.

"How you doing, Duff?" Tump said.

"I'll make it. How'd you know where I was?"

"Marvelous Marvella. Called her and she's bright as a new nickel now that she's back in her bag. Listen, brother, can you come over?"

"Man, I'm in the middle of a little bit of shit here."

"Duffy, you been in shit since the first minute I met you."

"That ain't nothing but the truth."

Tump said, "I need a favor."

"What kind of favor?"

"I'll run it down to you when you get here."

"That'll be hard, Tump. I don't think I can make it."

"Make it, man. It ain't nothing heavy. But I need you here and I need you now."

"Look, I'll make it simple. I'm here with Tish and she . . . she needs to get out of here for a few days. Maybe more. So I've got to find her a place where she can lay up and cool out, a place nobody knows where she is. That's all I can tell you because that's all I know."

Tump was his friend and Duffy didn't like lying to him. Maybe he should tell him, tell him all of it. Tell him about hitting Jert in the ass with the board. Tell him about whipping Jert's car with an aerial. He needed to tell it to *somebody*.

"That makes it all perfect then, doesn't it?" Tump was saying through the phone, clearly pleased. "Bring her here, her and that young stud, Felix."

Duffy said: "I can't do that."

"I don't know why the hell not. I ain't got nothing but a whole *floor* here. Nothing but solid comfort, and if the two of you are still fucked up with each other, the place is big enough for her to get *lost*." He laughed his great laugh. "We may have to send up a fucking flare or else send out a hunting party just to find her."

"I'll have to talk to her. I don't know what she'll say. If it's no, I'll give you a call. Otherwise, I'll see you in a bit."

"Solid."

"You're starting to talk like a nigger, you know that?"

"God knows I been practicing long enough," Tump said and hung up.

Duffy had no idea how Tish would react to Tump's invitation, but he didn't know any other way to go about telling her except to put it straight.

"That was Tump Walker. He says we ought to come to his place. What he was suggesting was that we stay as long as we like."

Felix went onto the floor in a paroxysm of joy. "Super, super, super," he sang over and over again.

"Does he have the room?" she said. "I mean for all of us to stay there?"

"Tish, he's got the whole goddam floor of a building. There may be a lot of things he doesn't have, but room's not one of them."

"How did the two of you get so close so quickly?" she said.

"Because he's a great guy," screamed Felix, thrashing on the floor. "The greatest guy in the whole world!"

"Felix has it. There it is. He's a great guy. We seem to fit."

"We'll go look at it," she said. "I just want to feel safe."

Felix, who couldn't seem to get up, wrestled with himself on the floor. He screamed, "You wouldn't be as safe with the U.S. Marines! He's mob*ile*, ag*ile* and host*ile!*"

"Get off the floor, Felix," Tish said. "You look like you're having a fit."

"I am having a fit," screamed Felix. "All us pig toters have fits."

"Where did he learn to talk like that?" asked Tish.

Duffy looked at his son, who had quieted there on the floor under his father's gaze. "I think he's probably always talked like that. We just never noticed it."

"Duffy," said Tish, "I knew you were a strange man. But I think you are stranger than I ever imagined."

Duffy smiled at her. "Probably so. I think I'm stranger than I ever imagined."

"When you talk like that," she said, "it scares me."

"Not any more than it does me. Come on, I'll help you get your things.

From where he lay, Felix watched his parents quietly.

17

"Dying goldfish and a few dead cats ain't crazy, Duffy," said Tump. "Besides, old folks can't go crazy, not in the South they can't. In the South they're just That Way. Besides, think about it, think of your own life. Put next to the shit you've done, is dying goldfish and a few dead cats crazy?"

"We're not talking about my life. What we're talking about is a situation that won't work."

"Put next to some of the shit I've done," said Tump, "dying goldfish and a few dead cats ain't nothing."

They were sitting in the rolling water of the Jacuzzi, a bottle of Stolichnaya vodka within reach. Tump tipped the bottle into the glass Duffy was holding and took a little for himself. "Sip on that good shit, man, and listen on," said Tump. But he only started telling Duffy again what he had already told him. Tump's mother was flying in on a chartered light aircraft from Tupelo, Mississippi. Just got to wanting to see her boy and she was coming.

"Your mother is flying here on a fucking chartered airplane?" Duffy had asked when he first heard it.

"I put a little green in the bank for her to hold, Duff. It wouldn't be right for the baddest-assed running back in the NFL to let his old mama walk around short. And, you know, I want to see her. Love it when I go home. But she's hard to handle sometimes. In Tupelo she knows everybody and everybody knows her. Old ladies need old ladies and she's got'm at home, but what the hell am I going to do with her here in Gainesville, where I don't know but a few people and the ones I know I don't like. Except you." He gave Duffy a funny little smile that had a vodka buzz in it. "You my main man. So I said to myself, Tump, what you do is get Duffy's mama and your mama and bring'm over here to this big old pad and they'll just have a hell of a time. Be good for both of'm."

"It won't work," said Duffy. "I can think of about a dozen reasons right off why it won't."

"Try one on me."

"My mother never leaves her apartment."

"When did you ask her last?"

"I quit asking."

Tump shook his head and made a smacking noise with his lips. "I hope you ain't starting to disappoint me, boy. You quit asking your old mama out into the air and sunshine?"

That's when Duffy explained about the goldfish. Tump shook it off with his own story about his mama's cats.

"She's got about a million. And when one of'm dies . . . or three . . . she doesn't throw'm out. Just leaves'm lying around the house. That's because she loves'm, man. Loves'm just as much dead as she does alive. Can you dig it? What the fuck's a few dead cats? Sooner or later one of her old ladies comes by, or *somebody* comes by. The house is rotten with dead cats and everything gets cleaned up. I got people looking in on her just for the cats. What am I supposed to do? Tell my mama she can't have her cats? Put her in a home? Hell, no. She's fine. She just gets strange notions sometimes, like this airplane-to-Gainesville business. When she called me on the phone, she didn't say nothing but she was coming. I can't tell my mama she can't come to see me. Besides, I want to see her." And here he cocked his thumb and pointed a long finger at Duffy. "I know you here, I know your mama's here, I know I got this condo." He shrugged his wet, sloping shoulders, his chest leaping with ropes of muscles. "Why not?"

"Why not? Why *not?*" groaned Duffy. "Tip the bottle, Tump."

Tump took the bottle out of the bucket of ice and poured.

"It's the least of the problems, but Tish won't go for it either," said Duffy.

Tump said: "Didn't I take care of Tish when she come in here? Was that righteous or what?"

It was righteous was what it was. Beautiful too. You would have thought that he had known Tish all his life, and that she and Duffy had been planning for months to move in here with hair dryers and makeup kits and suitcases and all manner of other shit.

When Duffy rapped with the brass knocker, Tump had swept open the door, looked directly at Tish and said, "Welcome to this house. I hear things been a little tight. Well, you home free now." It was a grand gesture, but it seemed right when Tump did it, and it clearly shocked Tish to silence. Tump threw a suitcase under his left arm, put one in his left hand, and pulled Felix off the floor in the crook of his right elbow and squeezed him. He looked at Felix, who was squirming with delight, and said: "I'd kiss you, but us hardasses don't kiss." Then he laughed and kissed him right on the mouth.

Tish and Duffy followed him down a hall and then off to the right to a self-contained wing: large, airy bedroom, dressing room, private bath with sunken tub, and a forest of incredibly green houseplants. There was a television set in the wall, an elaborate sound system and a wet bar.

He put the suitcases down and set Felix on the king-size bed. As naturally as if she had been his sister, he turned to Tish and took each of her thin shoulders in his massive hands and said: "You need anything, you just call on Tump. What about it? Make you a drink or maybe a little food? Anything?"

"I want to get in the bed and go to sleep," Tish said in the smallest of voices.

Tump turned to Felix and Duffy. "You guys heard the lady."

And he led the way back out into the living room, where Felix fell asleep on the couch while Tump was saying that they had to kick back and cool out before they talked about anything. Felix was softly snoring as Tump stood looking down at him. "Boy ain't used to running stadiums the whole night long, is he? What do you say, Duff—you up for a little Jacuzzi-cum-vodka, as us French niggers say?"

Tump poured Duffy just a touch more vodka. "You let me worry about things. I'll take care of everything like I took care of Tish when she came through the door."

"You did that as well as it could have been done, I'll give you that. But like I said, she won't go for my mother being over here, even if we could get that dear old lady out of her apartment, which we can't."

"Damn, son, you've started to repeat yourself. I heard all that the first time you said it."

"I'm catching a buzz off this vodka," said Duffy.

"Well, get your ass straight, because we got to meet a plane—that is, if you ain't expecting a call from Jane Fonda or some other pressing business."

"I've been expecting Jane to call," said Duffy, swirling the last of the vodka in the bottom of his glass, "but I don't think she'll call today."

Tump lifted himself out of the water and toweled down. He slipped into beltless powder-blue slacks and a short-sleeved linen shirt. He was moving with great purpose, and Duffy said, "Where you going?"

"First things first," said Tump. "Talk to Tish." He paused with his right foot in a leather moccasin. "Unless you mind."

"Hell, I don't mind."

When Tump was gone, he tipped the vodka bottle again, knowing this was the last drink for a while. He had to get his head right regardless of what Tish did or did not do. Tish. He was the one that should be talking to her. Or maybe not talking, just telling. Tell her he was the one in the room with Jert and her. He'd never seen her so rattled. Scared shitless, actually. And he hated that he didn't love her fear, but he didn't.

"Hey, come on, man. Stop with that vodka and get your ass out of there."

Duffy looked up at Tump and finished the glass. "What'd she say?"

"It's cool."

"What's cool?"

"Everything."

"Jesus, what did you tell her?"

"The truth. I told her who was coming here and why. And that I needed her help. That was what I told her first and last, that I needed her. It's cool. Get your ass out of there."

While Duffy was dressing, Tump asked, "Is there a store in town where we can get some good stuff like pig ears, maybe a few feet, some hog's head cheese, and fresh vegetables? I got to get something in here mama can cook with."

"I know a place across town. I've seen signs in the window. They sell that shit. They got the whole thing, from the tail to the snout."

As they were about to leave, Tump looked at Felix. "You think he'll be all right there?"

"There's a lot I might not know about Felix, but I know this. He'll be knocked out on that couch until somebody gets him off it."

They stood watching the boy where he snored softly, curled with his knees almost to his chest. "He's a good boy, Felix is," said Tump.

"Yeah, he is," said Duffy.

The parking lot was a blaze of late afternoon sun. Heat waves rose out of the macadam, causing the cars parked there to bend and dance. Duffy started toward his camper, but Tump caught his arm. "Let's take this."

Tump unlocked a Lincoln Town Car. Pulling into the street, Duffy said: "This is like riding in a goddam house. At least I can sleep and shit in mine."

"This ain't mine. It's . . ."

"I know. Part of the deal."

Tump flashed his smile. "How you feeling, Duff? Maybe you should have blown a little crank to cut back through that alcohol."

"Fuck the alcohol and fuck the crank. I'm fine."

"That's my man. Know when to use it and know when to lose it. Maybe we can go for a run later."

"Maybe."

But Duffy knew that was a lie. He was too whacked to do anything but try to maintain. Just maintaining would be triumph enough. He was a long way from having his head together. The program here was one thing at a time. Deal with the next thing in front of you. That was the program.

George's Market was not very big, not air-conditioned, and smelled of fresh-dug dirt. Duffy and Tump were standing in the back of the store, in front of a long display case of meat. A butcher in a bloody apron stood on the other side of it, watching them.

"You ever eat any backbone and rice?" asked Tump.

"What kind of backbone?" asked Duffy.

"Pork."

"I don't eat all that fried shit, Tump. You know that. Too much grease."

"You know what Satchel Paige said when they asked him about living long and staying strong? He said, 'Don't eat nothing that ain't fried.' That's what Satchel said, and even if he didn't say it, we got to go heavy to swine. My mama wouldn't know what to do in a kitchen that didn't have swine in it."

"Get what you need, man, and let's get out of here."

Duffy didn't want to look at the meat behind the glass anymore, the pig tails and jowls and ears and tripe.

"How 'bout tongue, Duff? That's beef. Let's get a couple of those tongues."

The tongues were curled like rattlesnakes behind the glass. They were dark and tapered away from the pointed tip to the thickness of a man's wrist. Duffy stared at them. The things must have been rooted down the throat of the cow. Duffy could see the tongues being torn out of the living bleeding animal, could see the blood spurting, although he knew that was nonsense, knew the animal was safely dead by the time it got around to losing its tongue. But he saw it anyway.

"I never had any," said Duffy.

"Good stuff. Chews like steak." He motioned to the butcher. "Give us two of those tongues. No, make it three."

"You ever think about death, Tump?"

Tump turned slowly to look at him. "Everybody thinks about death."

"What do *you* think?"

"You serious?"

"Yeah. What do you think when you think about it?"

"*Damn*, Duffy." But Duffy only looked at him. "I think," said Tump, "that . . . that . . . I think death will annoy me." The butcher threw the tongue on the counter in front of Tump. "And five pounds of backbone."

"Annoy? Annoy, for Christ's sake. You think that?"

"You asked me. I told you. The thing that pisses me off is that you got to die in the middle of something, you dig? Unfinished. You pick up a fine-looking bitch in a bar and you're on the way to her apartment to get in her pants and you get run over by a truck. That's annoying. Yeah. Or you order the best steak in a place and while it's on the way to your table, you pitch forward in your salad, dead. That's annoying. Don't look at me like that. I ain't shucking and I ain't playing with you. That's the way I think about it."

"That's a fucking joke."

"Yeah, and it's on you, sucker, death is." He took the backbone from the butcher and dropped it into the loaded cart. "I'll tell you something else, since you had to bring this shit up. I've seen myself breaking into the open field with the ball, I've beat everybody and I'm going for the end zone, just streaking . . . and my goddam heart stops." Tump had gradually leaned more into Duffy's face, his own face going hard under his flat, bright eyes, his voice dropping, becoming hoarser. "Fucking ball goes one way, I go the other, and I'm dead." Their noses were almost touching by the time Tump said the last word. Anybody looking at them from across the store would have thought they were about to fight. They hung like that a moment, silent, then Tump slowly smiled, blinked and said, "Wouldn't that just annoy the shit out of me?" He straightened, caught Duffy's shoulder and shook it. "Now let's take a flier from this subject for a while." He wheeled the cart toward the checkout counter, Duffy beside him.

Duffy said: "Didn't mean to piss you off. Maybe it's the vodka."

"You haven't pissed anybody off, man. But I come in here to buy swine for my mama's kitchen and you put death on me. That's cold."

"I guess it is," said Duffy.

18

They were standing in the parking lot, putting Tump's mother's bag in the trunk. She was already in the car, an enormous, very black woman in a yellow dress and yellow shoes and carrying a yellow purse.

Tump started sniffing and asked, "You smell something, Duffy?"

"Smell what?"

"Something that doesn't smell right. Smells wrong. Real wrong." He eyed a wicker basket that closed with a lid held by a leather buckle. He leaned forward and opened it. A large cat lay curled up and dead in the bottom of the basket.

"Suffering God of us all," said Duffy.

Tump lifted the cat out of the basket and held it out toward Duffy. "My sweet, dear mama and her goddam pets," said Tump.

"Throw that thing away before I lose my vodka."

"It ain't nothing but a dead cat," Tump said, "kitten, really. Here, look at it."

Duffy had turned his back. "I don't want to look at it."

"Squeamish fucker," said Tump. He dropped the cat and threw the rest of the stuff in the trunk.

"Git in here, Jerome," his mother called. "I'm burning up."

Duffy turned to look at him. "Jerome?"

"You don't think any mama in Tupelo, Mississippi, would ever name her son Tump, do you?"

They got in and Tump turned on the air conditioning. "That do feel good to us old folks," his mother said.

Duffy turned to look at her in the back seat. She was smiling and her mouth was a wonder of gold.

"It's hotter here than it is at home, Mama," Tump said.

"This is Florida, child, it's supposed to be hot." She cut her eyes to Duffy. "So you a lawyer. My, my, ain't that nice. Use to think Jerome gone be a lawyer when he was little. He was the talkingest youngun God ever smiled on. Yes."

"He's done fine," Duffy said. "You wouldn't want him to be a lawyer, Mrs. Walker."

"Pearl, you call me Pearl. And, yeah, my Jerome's done fine. I always known he would. A good boy too. He never brought me no grief."

"Now, Mama," said Tump.

"Ain't nothing but the truth," she said.

Duffy watched Pearl, who had brought a paper fan from somewhere, a fan with the face of Jesus on it, and was fanning herself with it. Despite the air conditioning, her great dark face ran with sweat.

"You'll be cooler when we get to the apartment." Duffy only spoke to have something to say, because she was looking at him with eyes that seemed at once intimate and conspiratorial.

"Lord," she said, "I don't git no cooler than this. I commence sweatin' in May and don't stop till September."

Duffy wanted to talk to her about the cats, about the cat they had found in the basket. He would have really liked that. She certainly didn't seem as fucked up as his mother. She did, in fact, seem downright normal. He did not know what he expected, but he had not expected normal. Carrying a dead cat around was not normal. It was mad. Craziness.

On the drive home, she pawed around through the sacks of groceries beside her in the back seat. Tump explained to her that the sweet potatoes and the new potatoes were dug right out

144

of the surrounding countryside, and that the summer squash and tomatoes and pole beans were trucked in fresh today.

"I have to come cook for him, Duffy," she said. "If I don't come cook for this boy, he falls off to nothing but breath and britches."

"Now, Mama," Tump said.

"Ain't nothing but the truth," she said. She leaned forward and looked up at the sky. "It was so beautiful up there today. You boys should have been with me. So peaceful, nothing but blue sky and me sailing through it like a bird. I could've gone on forever."

"You like to fly, Pearl?" asked Duffy. His own mother would not fly. Duffy had always thought it was because his father was shot down, but he didn't know for sure. He and his mother had never talked about it.

"Would you believe I never flown until I was fifty years old?" she said. "Scared to death the first time Jerome taken and flown me. But after that first time I took to it like it was a natural thing."

"Mama can't get enough of flying," said Tump. "One of these days, I'm going to get a call and she'll be in Japan or somewheres."

"Boy, don't josh you mama," she said, leaning forward to smack him on his shoulder with her fan. "Airplanes pleasure me. Something wrong with that?"

"Not a thing, Mama," Tump said, "not a thing."

In the parking lot at Tump's place, Pearl grabbed the wicker basket out of the trunk of the car and headed for the sparse shade of a palm tree, her monstrous hips heaving under her yellow dress. "I got to get out of this sun," she called over her shoulder, "before I'm heat struck. Jerome, you got to get you a hat."

As they were getting her bags out, Duffy said, "What's she going to say when she finds the cat missing?"

"Nothing. She mislays a lot of things, or as she says, misputs a lot of things. When the cat's not there, she'll just think she misput him."

Tump opened the apartment door for his mother, who took a quick look around and said, "Jerome, you live in the beatinest places. But this one beats *everything*."

"I hope you don't mind me being here." The three of them turned to see Jert McPhester rising out of an overstuffed chair in a far corner, by the glass door giving onto the balcony. "I . . . ah . . . just . . . ah . . . needed a place to sit for a while. Things got so rank I couldn't tell if I was coming or going."

"I can tell," said Duffy. "You're going."

"Hush, Duffy," said Tump. "Tish let you in, did she?"

"She's asleep, at least she was the last time I looked. It was actually Marvella who let me in."

"Marvella?" said Duffy.

"She's in the Jacuzzi," Jert said.

"*Was* in the Jacuzzi," said Marvella, coming into the room. She was wearing a bikini that didn't have enough cloth in it to make a glove out of. It looked as if it was held on by suction.

"Well now," said Pearl, "ain't you a pretty thing."

"Mama, this is Marvella Sweat. Marvella, meet my mama, Pearl."

"Sweat? Why, it's a crowd of Sweats in Mississippi. I wouldn't misdoubt I know some of you kinfolk."

"There's Sweats all over Mississippi and Alabama—that's where I'm from—and Georgia."

"Son, I believe you made real nice friends here in Gainesville."

Marvella went to Pearl and threw her arm around her shoulder and shook her gently. "You're an ole sweetheart is what you are." Marvella sniffed violently and sucked clear liquid off her upper lip. "Let's party."

"We're going in the kitchen and cook up a mess of supper is what we're going to do," Pearl said.

"My appetite's been off," said Marvella, her bright eyes darting from face to face, her expression unchanged.

Stoned witless, thought Duffy. Where in the hell would all this take them? Something felt as if it was getting out of hand.

Jert, who had been shifting from foot to foot over by the glass door, said, "My name's Jert McPhester. I'm Tump's lawyer . . . and his friend."

"My boy's name is Jerome. Tump? What kind of name is that? Only a fool would name her youngun Tump, and I ain't no fool. I look like a fool to you?"

"No, ma'm," Jert said.

Tump smiled at Duffy. "Right feisty, ain't she? Marvella, put these groceries in the kitchen while I get Mama settled."

"I don't even like to *handle* food," Marvella said.

"I'll help you," said Jert.

"I need a drink," Duffy said.

"Come on, Mama, back this way. Go light on that stuff, Duff."

Duffy said: "I don't think light will get it."

"My God," Marvella was saying from the kitchen. "Jert, what is this shit?"

"Those are pig ears, darling," Jert said. "I thought you were from Alabama."

"Birmingham. I'm from Birmingham. We don't eat pig ears in Birmingham."

"That's not what I heard," said Jert. "I heard you eat *any-thing* in Birmingham."

Marvella gave a high squeal and punched Jert in the arm. "You big old *thang*."

Duffy went back to Tish's bedroom, through the forest of houseplants, uncapped a bottle of whiskey at the bar and poured himself a drink. He had consciously avoided looking at the bed, but as soon as he walked into the room, he heard the gentle, wet snoring of Felix. He knocked the drink back, poured himself another, and then turned to look at the bed, where Felix slept hugging a pillow beside his mother. Tish had apparently washed her hair and it was soft and bright, and curled now across her cheek and down her neck. Her lips were slightly parted, showing her white perfect teeth.

Mother. Son. Family. A fucking Norman Rockwell painting, thought Duffy. He wondered why everybody bought it, believed it. "Because we're all hopelessly in love with the smell of shit," he said softly. But even as he said it, he didn't believe himself. He hoped desperately that he was wrong. The evidence, though, did not support Norman Rockwell. The evidence of Duffy's own life suggested something quite different. Maybe that said more about his life than it did about anything else. The flush of the whiskey warmed his face and made him feel a little more optimistic. He took another drink, sighed, and decided that he didn't have to worry about it.

"Hey, Duffy." Tump's whispered voice came to him from the doorway. Duffy followed him out into the living room. "Let's go see your mama."

"We've got enough people in here to fight a war already," said Duffy. "Where's Jert and Marvella?"

Tump shrugged. "Here somewhere. You're not hanging up on me, are you?"

"I'm not hanging up on anybody."

"Good. That's my man. We'll take my car."

On the elevator going down to the parking lot, Tump asked Duffy what he was doing back there in Tish's room, and when Duffy said he was getting a drink, Tump asked him why he had not drunk from the bottle in the living room.

"I was looking at her. At her and Felix."

"Looking at her?"

"Right."

Tump sucked his teeth and then whistled a little tune and didn't say anything else until they were headed west on University Avenue. The traffic was light, since most of the university students were gone for the summer, but Tump drove slowly, apparently in no hurry.

"Say, Duff, you still pissed with Jert about losing a tooth at the handball court?"

"I don't even think about it."

"Then what's the hard-on about? The one you got for Jert?"

"It's complicated."

"Tell me to drop it and it's done. But I hate to see your head messed up the way it's been since . . . since I first met you."

"It's a long story."

"I got time. If you ever need to tell me, just remember, I got time."

"I always felt like a man ought to keep his story to himself. You carry your own shit in this world."

"That wouldn't be the first thing you've been wrong about." A long pause, then: "Would it?" Tump said.

Duffy opened his mouth to say something but only groaned. The sound startled him, as though it was coming out of somebody else's mouth. And out of the groan, the words started, the story.

As best as he could, he told all of it, starting slowly, not sure he wanted to do it. But finding great relief in the telling, he talked faster and faster. It took a long time and Tump never interrupted. He drove slowly and kept his eyes on the road, for which Duffy was grateful. When it was all out, a silence fell between them.

Then finally, still without looking at him, Tump said: "You whipped the man's car?"

"That's what I did."

"But you were drunk then."

"I wasn't until I started whipping it. The longer I whipped, it seemed like the drunker I got."

"Squeezed his balls and made him crow like a rooster. Bought you some camouflaged pants. Put shoe polish on your face." Tump's voice was soft, bemused, as though he was ticking it all off on his fingers. "Broke into your own house. Hit the man in the ass with a board while he was tooling your old lady."

Duffy didn't answer. He watched a young man and a young woman on the sidewalk. They were wearing matching maroon

T-shirts. The man's shirt had a 1 on the back. The girl's had a 2. They were holding hands.

"Whooeee, damn!" said Tump, smacking the steering wheel with his palm.

He could feel Tump watching him, but Duffy kept his eyes on the road. A strange and pleasant calm had descended upon him. The afternoon sky was beautiful over Payne's Prairie.

"At least you don't have to feel weird about sick goldfish and dead cats anymore," said Tump. "They ain't shit beside whipping cars. Or camouflaging up for a raid on your own bedroom."

"The strangest part of it all is that I didn't give a shit," said Duffy. "That's what Zen is all about. The good with the bad. The great *One*. That's my mom's place up there on the right. Golden House."

"I don't know what Zen is all about, but I been around the block enough to know bullshit when I hear it. A man that don't give a shit walks away. Peeping and creeping is not his style. Or whipping up on cars. Think about it."

"I don't want to think about it."

"You ought to. That's something you ought to think about." Tump pulled into the parking space nearest the entrance to Golden House. As they went up to her apartment, Duffy asked, "What'll you tell her?"

"Tell her?"

"What are you going to *say?*"

"I'm inviting the lady to dinner, Duffy. What's the problem?"

Duffy didn't answer but stopped in front of a door with a brass goldfish on it. There was a small card in a metal holder under the goldfish: MRS. HENRY DEETER.

Duffy rang the bell, and almost immediately the door swung open.

"Glad you came," said Duffy's mother. She was wearing a brown sweater buttoned to the throat and had a knitted brown shawl across her thin shoulders. "I called your damn house but nobody answered. And I think your secretary may be losing her mind." Her eyes swung from Duffy to Tump. "Who the hell are you?"

"This is a good friend of mine, Mom. He—"

"My name's Jerome Walker."

"You a lawyer?"

"No, ma'm, I'm not," Tump said.

"Good. Most lawyers would rather climb a tree and tell a lie than stand on flat ground and tell the truth. Never met a lawyer I liked. Except Duffy, and he pisses me off about half the time. You've got your full growth, though. That's good. You never know when you're going to need a little heft. Heft never hurts. Well, don't just stand there, come on in." They stepped through the door and she closed it. She turned to Tump. "What I noticed is, they've got goldfish just like I do."

"They do?" Tump said.

"Just look around you," she said.

Tump looked around the living room at the goldfish, swimming lethargically through cloudy water in bowls lining the walls and sitting on the tables at the ends of the couch.

"And I thought what we better do," she said, "is find out how long they're going to let me stay here."

Duffy looked at Tump, sighed, and said, "She got that from my father. Apparently it runs in the family. You can see the problem."

"Got what from your father?" demanded his mother. "There won't be a problem if we can find out how long they're going to let me stay."

"Mom," sighed Duffy, "you don't have a thing to worry about. We talked to them and they said you could stay here as long as you like."

"You're not just pissing on my foot and calling it rain, are you?"

"Tell her, Tump," said Duffy.

"Duffy's right, Mrs. Deeter," Tump said, without missing a beat. "We did have a talk with them. They're reasonable and good people. And they said you can stay here as long as you like."

"No problem," said Duffy.

"And on top of that," said Tump, "we wanted to know if you'd like to come over to my place for some home cooking. Nobody over there but friends and family."

She gathered her shawl more tightly about her shoulders as she looked about the room from one line of cloudy bowls to the next. "Maybe they'll change the water for these fucking fish while I'm gone." She went over to her chair by the window and started pulling on a long cloth coat.

"Tump," said Duffy. "You're wasting yourself playing football. You ought to run for President."

19

The air was blue with smoke when they got back to Tump's condominium. Jert and Marvella were on their knees on the living room floor, a bamboo bong between them.

"We found your stash, Tump," said Marvella. "I had to have something to get off this mountain."

"It's cool with me," said Tump. "I jack my blood up now and then, but I never burn my lungs. Don't use the stuff. Came with the place."

Mrs. Deeter looked around slowly, staring hard at everything, and then said, "Jerome, is what you do against the law?"

"No, ma'm. Not against the law, just in short supply. Mrs. Deeter, I'd like you to meet Marvella and . . ."

The old lady snorted. "I know Jert already. A fucking lawyer. And I've heard of Marvella." She walked over to where Marvella was kneeling. "You're a skinny little thing, but I hear tell the closer the bone, the sweeter the meat. So many women and so little time, right, Duffy?"

"For God's sake, Mom!"

"Somebody's cooking something," Duffy's mother said.

Tump said, "That's my mama, she . . ."

But Mrs. Deeter was already headed for the kitchen, apparently following the smell of food, sniffing and snorting as she went.

As Tump and Duffy followed her, Tump said, "You got a great mama, man. She cuts right through the bullshit. You ought to be proud of her."

Duffy smiled. "She raised me, didn't she?"

"You like yourself too much, Duffy."

"If I don't like myself, who the hell would?"

"Not many that I've seen so far," said Tump.

Something must have showed in Duffy's face, something that translated out of the knot that jerked in his stomach, because Tump threw his arm around his shoulders and said, "Hey, Felix and I love you."

Pearl had changed out of her yellow dress and shoes into a housedress with a kind of apron attached to the front and a pair of heelless slippers. The entire top of the stove was covered with bubbling pots and Felix was sitting in the corner with a plate in his lap. The plate was piled with something Duffy didn't recognize.

Mrs. Deeter rushed to the stove, lifted a lid and spoke into the rising steam. "I'm Myrtle Deeter," she shouted.

Mrs. Walker flashed a brilliant smile, looked up from the bowl of dough she was kneading and said just as loudly, "I'm Jerome's mama, name Pearl. Duffy must be your boy."

"I'm guilty of that," she said, lifting another lid from a bubbling pot. "What've you got going here, anyway?"

"Some of this and some of that, just cooking up a *mess* of stuff," said Pearl.

Duffy wondered why they were shouting. Maybe they were just nervous. Pearl looked at Duffy. "You got the eatingest boy I seen since Jerome was his size."

"He'll eat anything he can chew up," said Myrtle. "Takes that from his granddaddy, he does."

Tump moved closer to Duffy. "See how they sliding through this, man. Old ladies have done seen all the ways a day can do.

154

They're tougher than you and I'll ever be. They slide through stuff that would kill us."

"What's that Felix is eating?" Duffy said.

"One of my favorites, Duff. Try a piece."

"Try it, Dad," said Felix. "This'll put fuel in the ole tank if anything will."

Duffy picked a piece off Felix's plate. It was cut into inch squares, crisp and white. He popped it in his mouth and chewed. "Pork," said Duffy, but kept chewing.

"Pig ears, actually," said Tump.

Pig ears were definitely a challenge. A man had to by God have *enthusiasm* to get through a pig ear. Besides, it was good. Obviously deep fried, a little like pork rind.

"You like it, don't you?" said Tump.

Duffy didn't answer, but took another piece and put it in his mouth. If this was pig ear eating time, then by God he could do it with the best of them.

"You're a good man, Duffy, but you're willful. I got a feeling you missed a whole lot of good things in your life because you decided too much ahead of time."

Pearl said: "Honey, get out of that coat before you keel over with heat stroke."

"I might drop like a shot bird one day, but it won't be from heat. It'll be from air conditioning. Air conditioners are not natural."

"I'm a natural-born sweater, myself. I'd sweat if I was a Eskimo."

Jert came into the kitchen. He didn't look good. His skin was gray and he seemed to be chewing the insides of his mouth. "Smells good in here," he said, but his voice didn't sound as if he meant it. Duffy figured Marvella had run some coke up his nose.

Myrtle snorted. "Jert McPhester, you'd think shit smelled good."

Pearl turned from the stove. "Whoooeee, chile, you do got a *mouth* on you."

"It's nothing but the truth. And I believe in the truth."

"Sister woman, I do too." She looked up from the bread she was spooning into deep fat. "The truth, I say the *very* truth."

"The truth," said Myrtle, "will make you feel like you're in hell with your back broke. The truth will, if you're not careful."

"Ah," Pearl said, rolling her eyes and speaking to the ceiling. "But we careful with the truth."

Duffy said to Tump: "We're getting into just what I thought we'd get into here."

"Getting into what, Duff? Relax man, and go with it."

"Say, Tump," said Jert, "you mind if I cool out in your Jacuzzi for a while? I'm not feeling so hot."

"Maybe you ought to split," Tump said. "Go back to your place and kick back, you know?"

Duffy put his hand on Tump's arm. "No, no, stick around, Jert. Get into the Jacuzzi. Sure, that'll do you good."

"I was thinking the same thing."

When he was gone, Tump said, "Now what the hell was that all about?"

"I don't know," said Duffy. Then: "Yet."

Over the steaming stove, Duffy's mother had brought up the subject of goldfish.

"Goldfish?" said Pearl, stirring an open pot.

"You ever keep 'm?" demanded Myrtle.

"I'm not going to listen to this," said Duffy. "I *can't* listen to this. Do something for me, will you, Tump?"

"Anything at all, Duff."

"Take care of Marvella for me."

"What do you mean, take care of her? What am I supposed to do with her?"

"You been fucked recently?" said Duffy.

"Duffy Deeter," said Tump, not smiling, "you are sometimes a sorry sonofabitch."

"Sometimes I am," said Duffy, and walked out of the kitchen.

Marvella was still in the living room when Duffy went through, her mouth on the bong, her cheeks caved in, sucking for all she was worth. She didn't even look up, and Duffy was grateful for that. On the way back to Tish's bedroom he could hear the water of the Jacuzzi. Only when he heard the water did he realize that he was murderously angry, and more than that, he realized that he didn't even know what he was angry at or with. Jert? Tish? Himself? All three at once? The whole fucking world maybe? He didn't know.

Tish was sitting at a dressing table in front of a mirror, brushing her hair. She glanced at him briefly and went on stroking her hair. He went to the bar and poured himself a drink.

"Don't you think you've had enough of that?" she said.

"I've had enough of everything."

"What's that supposed to mean?"

"Exactly what I said. Are you going to stay back here forever?"

"Maybe. Maybe I am."

"What bullshit!" Only after the words were out did he realize he was shouting.

Tish quit with the brush and turned to face him. There were tears in her eyes.

"You don't understand a thing, do you?" she said, in a voice that reminded him of when he had first met her, when he had first loved her. "I've been run out of my own house. I've had the natural Jesus scared out of me, and all you can do is scream at me." Now she was crying.

He wanted to go to her, to hold her. But he could not. He didn't pour another drink but just turned up the bottle and bubbled it twice.

"Let me make it easy for you," he said. "Nobody robbed you and Jert, and nobody pistol whipped him. It wasn't like that at all."

Her crying stopped and a flush spread over her cheeks. "I don't know how you found out, but, no, it wasn't like that. It was worse. It was a lot worse."

"Tish, I don't think you and I ever told each other the truth about anything, nothing at all."

In a very small voice, she said, "I couldn't tell you."

"No, you couldn't. Because you didn't know."

"Know what?"

"I did it. I did it all, Tish."

"You . . ."

"I hit Jert in the ass with my old fraternity paddle. Twice, when he was in bed with you. I went to the parking lot of the Hilton at three o'clock in the morning and beat the shit out of his car with the aerial I ripped off it." He took another quick hit from the bottle. "He's out there in the Jacuzzi right now. You want to join him? Go. Nobody'll stop you and nobody'll say a word about it."

He didn't know how he expected her to react, but he certainly didn't expect laughter, a high, almost hysterical laughter, while tears started again down her cheeks. She got up from the dressing table and came to him. The only thing he could think she possibly meant to do was strike him. And he meant to take it. He honestly felt he ought to be struck. But instead she folded herself into him in a way that he could never remember her doing before and kissed him, her tongue alive in his mouth. Then she drew her face away and said, "McPhester is a jerk."

"A jerk," he said, "that I hit in the ass with a board while he was fucking you."

"Lao-tse would say that doesn't make me bad, it only makes me human. At least that's what you told me. Taught me . . . tried to teach me."

"I don't know that I believed any of it. I don't know if I believe anything. Maybe everything I've ever said or ever done has been a lie. I don't know why I've done anything I've done." Now he was crying. He could feel the tears running on his face. He couldn't remember this kind of total, hopeless weeping since he was a child. He felt utterly lost. He reached for the whiskey bottle, but Tish put her hand on his wrist and stopped him. She drew him to her, and now he was sobbing uncontrollably.

"You poor sweet baby," she said. "You poor fucked-up darling. You don't need the whiskey. I've got something better."

And in the miraculous motion that only women know when they truly want to get out of their clothes, her dressing gown was gone and she was naked, leading him to the bed. How he got out of his own clothes he would never remember. The memory that would stay with him was that at some moment he was riding the high crest of her passion that was better than anything he had ever done, better than anything he had ever thought he believed, better than anything he had ever wanted. And when it was done they lay like two sweated, exhausted children.

He looked at her with dazed eyes in a kind of wonder. "Well," he said.

"Well," she said.

"I never knew you," he said.

"We never knew each other," she said.

"Are we still going on the goddam trip? The Winnebago's packed just like we had it, and it's downstairs."

She touched his lips with her fingers. "Duffy Deeter," she said. "You've got that look on your face again."

"What look is that?"

"I always thought of it as evil, an evil grin."

"That's enthusiasm, darlin'. It's only when I really want something."

"What do you want? Right this minute, what?"

"To get you and old Felix and go down somewhere in south Florida, somewhere in Miami to one of those great hotels, and lie up for about a week together and see what we can put back together."

"Do you think we've got anything to put together?"

"How the hell should I know? But we'll never know if we don't go give it a shot. You up for it? You game?"

"Try me," she said.

"Get your shit together and let's get out of here." He bounded out of the bed.

"Duffy?" He stopped at the foot of the bed, pulling on his jeans. "What are you going to do?"

"I was thinking about killing Jert before we left, but I'm just going to see Tump."

"He's quite somebody, Tump is, isn't he?"

"He is that. Tump don't fit nobody's mold."

"Attorneys shouldn't use grammar like that."

"Maybe that's not what I am, or ever was. If we knew who I was or how we fit together, we wouldn't need to take the trip, would we? Now, are you going to roll out of those sheets and let's move it, or what?"

"You're talking in that old voice again," she said.

"What the fuck did you expect? That I'd suddenly be somebody else? I won't. And you won't. And old Felix won't, who, by the way, is probably the best thing we ever did together. But at least we won't lie anymore or fuck with each other's head anymore. All right?"

She was smiling and beautiful and naked as she rose from the bed. "Right," she said.

When Duffy went back into the living room, Tump was standing there, his hands on his hips, as though he might have been waiting there this whole time.

Tump said: "You got something right, didn't you, Buckshot?"

"How the hell did you know that?"

"It's in your face."

"I got a toehold, buddy. Not a handle, but at least something. Tish and I are heading south."

Tump smiled. "Jesus, that's what she said you'd be doing."

"Who said?"

"Marvella. She split. She said to tell you that she thanked you for the party. Quite a girl, that Marvella. Too bad you never got to know her. She was never the airhead you thought she was."

"I never said she was an airhead."

"No, you never *said* it."

"Don't rain on me, man. I can't stand any more rain right at the moment."

Tump reached up and took him by both shoulders. "Keep your head up, champ. You're going to be fine."

"Do you think I ought to drown Jert in the Jacuzzi?"

"Is that what you feel like doing?"

"No. I don't want to do anything to Jert. He's not the problem. He never was. An asshole, yes. But not the problem."

Tump put his arm across Duffy's shoulders. "Come in here and let me show you something."

He led Duffy into the dining room, where his mother and Tump's mother had covered the table with bowls of steaming food. Felix was already at a plate, sawing with a knife and forking something fried into his mouth.

"Dad," said Felix, "you ever eat any tripe?"

"I never did, son."

"Well, get a plate and get to it. Let's all stoke the old machine."

Tump said: "That boy was born to tote the pig."

"Tell it, Tump! Tell it!" said the boy, forking more meat into his working jaws.

Duffy's mother came in from the kitchen and demanded, "Guess what?"

"I wouldn't even try, Mom."

"Pearl's coming over to see the hangar. She knows as much about airplanes as Henry did."

It was the first time he had heard his mother use his father's first name since he died.

"I sure am gone do that," said Pearl, coming up behind her. "I may never go back to Tupelo."

"See," said Tump. "See how everything works out?"

"Yeah," said Duffy. "I *do* see."